"Look at that.
It's beautiful, don't you think?"

Connor looked up, but he couldn't see the moon from where he was standing. He bent down and took a quick look. "Yeah, I guess so."

Sunny stood and beckoned him closer. "Look from over here," she said, moving toward the porch railing.

He hung back, not sure he should let himself get any closer. Any closer and his body would definitely be involved. "It's just the moon," he said, moving a little nearer. "No big deal."

Sunny took two large steps and gripped his hand. Tugging gently, she said, "Boy do you need to loosen up." When they reached the railing, she pointed up again, smiling. "There. Now look at that and tell me it's not beautiful."

"Beautiful," he murmured.

"I was talking about the moon."

"And I was talking about you."

Dear Reader,

When you're stuffing the stockings this year remember that Silhouette Romance's December lineup is the perfect complement to candy canes and chocolate! Remind your loved ones—and yourself—of the power of love.

Open your heart to magic with the third installment of IN A FAIRY TALE WORLD…, the miniseries where matchmaking gets a little help from an enchanted princess. In *Her Frog Prince* (SR #1746) Shirley Jump provides a rollicking good read with the antics of two opposites who couldn't be more attracted!

Then meet a couple of heartbreaking cowboys from authors Linda Goodnight and Roxann Delaney. In *The Least Likely Groom* (SR #1747) Linda Goodnight brings us a risk-taking rodeo man who finds himself the recipient of lots of tender loving care—from one very special nurse! And Roxann Delaney pairs a beauty disguised as an ugly duckling with the man most likely to make her smolder, in *The Truth About Plain Jane* (SR #1748).

Last but not least, discover the explosive potential of close proximity as a big-city physician works side by side with a small-town beauty. Is it her wacky ideas that drive him crazy—or his sudden desire to make her his? Find out in *Love Chronicles* (SR #1749) by Lissa Manley.

Watch for more heartwarming titles in the coming year. You don't want to miss a single one!

Happy reading!

Mavis C. Allen
Associate Senior Editor

Please address questions and book requests to:
Silhouette Reader Service
U.S.: 3010 Walden Ave., P.O. Box 1325, Buffalo, NY 14269
Canadian: P.O. Box 609, Fort Erie, Ont. L2A 5X3

Love Chronicles

LISSA MANLEY

SILHOUETTE *Romance*®

Published by Silhouette Books

America's Publisher of Contemporary Romance

This book is dedicated to my fantastic editor, Patience Smith. Your input and editorial advice have made my books so much better. Thank you.

SILHOUETTE BOOKS

ISBN 0-373-19749-7

LOVE CHRONICLES

Copyright © 2004 by Melissa A. Manley

This edition published by arrangement with Harlequin Books S.A.

® and TM are trademarks of Harlequin Books S.A., used under license. Trademarks indicated with ® are registered in the United States Patent and Trademark Office, the Canadian Trade Marks Office and in other countries.

Visit Silhouette Books at www.eHarlequin.com

Printed in U.S.A.

Books by Lissa Manley

Silhouette Romance

The Bachelor Chronicles #1665
The Bridal Chronicles #1689
The Baby Chronicles #1705
Love Chronicles #1749

LISSA MANLEY

has been an avid reader of romance since her teens and firmly believes that writing romances with happy endings is her dream job. She lives in the beautiful Pacific Northwest with her college-sweetheart husband of nineteen years, Kevin, two children, Laura and Sean, and two feisty toy poodles named Lexi and Angel, who run the household and get away with it. She has a degree in business from the University of Oregon, having discovered the joys of writing well after her college years. In her spare time, she enjoys reading, crafting, attending her children's sporting events and relaxing at the family vacation home on the Oregon coast.

Lissa loves to hear from her readers. She can be reached at P.O. Box 91336, Portland, OR 97291-0336, or at http://lissamanley.com.

Dear Mr. Commitment,

My husband forgot our anniversary this year. He spends more time in the garage with his precious lawn tools than with me. What can I do to spice up our love life?

Yours sincerely,
Out of it in Oregon

Dear Out of it,

To spice up your love life, put more cayenne in his chili. Not only will he notice you, but it will knock the stuffing out of him! Ha ha ha!

Mr. Commitment

Dear Out of it,

Forget what Mr. Commitment says! To spice up your love life, do one little romantic thing each day to show him how much you love him. In the meantime, sign up for a class, take tap lessons, audition for a town play—find your own "precious lawn tools."

Best of luck!
Sunny Williams

Chapter One

Connor Forbes glanced up from the medical journal he was reading at the receptionist's counter and looked at the office window.

"What a crock," he grumbled, staring at the words *Mr. Commitment* painted in gold letters below his father's name, Brady Forbes, M.D. Unfortunately, Connor's name would soon take the place of his father's and the whole town of Oak Valley, Oregon, would be coming to him not only for their medical problems, which he was more than qualified to handle, but for their relationship problems, too.

He snorted and shook his head, then rubbed his eyes under his wire-rimmed reading glasses. A man who'd failed to keep a girlfriend for more than three months at a time was the last person who should be Mr. Commitment.

He dropped his hands from his eyes and his dire thoughts were cut off when a large, black-and-white blur ran by the office's floor-to-ceiling window. Drawing his eyebrows together, Connor straightened just as a slender woman dressed in a flowing skirt ran by. She was waving one hand in the air while the other clutched a large tote bag, her sunshine-blond hair streaming out behind her.

Intrigued—nothing remotely exciting ever happened in Oak Valley, and certainly nothing involving lithe, feminine legs and long, silky blond hair—he moved out from behind the desk and headed closer to the window to get a better view.

The blur reappeared across the street. Connor's eyebrows went up when he saw that the black-and-white thing was a giant dog running at breakneck speed down the boardwalk.

The runaway mutt took a sharp right and leaped off the boardwalk and into the street, his huge paws flopping, his whip-like tail held high in the air. Just about the time Connor thanked heaven traffic was nonexistent in Oak Valley, the dog headed straight toward his office. In one mighty leap, the crazy canine cleared the step up to the boardwalk. Tongue lolling, he took another step and then skidded to a halt just in time to plant his huge front paws on the window facing Connor. He let out a huge *woof,* his tail wagging, his mouth pressed into what Connor would swear was a doggy smile.

Before Connor could recover from the attack of the humongous smiling dog, the woman with the sunshine-blond hair ran up, her brows knitted together, her pink lips pressed into a frown. She had high cheekbones and what looked like a smattering of freckles on her perfect nose. She wore a long, flowing pink skirt and gauzy white top.

She dropped her bag, grabbed the dog's collar and pulled him off the window. She bent over, shaking a scolding finger at the delinquent mutt. Didn't seem to faze the animal in the least. He playfully jumped around, barking, trying to get loose.

After her "scolding," she hooked the leash on the dog, then straightened. She reached up with a noticeable huff and flipped her sunglasses onto the top of her head, exposing a strip of firm flesh at her waist where her top fell short.

Connor took his glasses off and stared, his blood heating up. She was beautiful. His last relationship, clocking in at a bare three weeks, had ended five months ago. He was due.

She turned his way and saw him, almost giving him a heart attack when her gorgeous topaz-brown gaze hit his. She stared back, the attraction clearly mutual; then her eyes refocused and she gazed at the words on the window. She mouthed the words *Mr. Commitment.*

He swore the flush on her cheeks deepened as she took in his white lab coat, then gave him a feeble little wave, as if it weren't okay to swap stares with a doctor. Shaking her head, she pulled the dog to one of the wooden benches that lined the boardwalk, tied him up and then, surprisingly, made her way back toward Connor's office.

Okay, maybe it *was* okay to stare at a doctor.

He returned to his spot behind the reception counter. June, his nurse/receptionist who would normally greet visitors, was having a problem getting her grandson to preschool and hadn't arrived yet.

As the mystery woman opened the door and stepped inside, he got hold of himself and knitted his brow. Who was she? Not a scheduled patient; he knew everyone who had appointments with him this morning. He didn't recognize her as a local, either. Although he *had* been in Seattle for a long time. Still, he'd been back for a month and he wouldn't forget a woman who looked like her. Not in a million years. Besides, if he did know her, he sure wouldn't be feeling a sharp lack of female companionship in his life right now.

Miss Sunshine stood on the other side of the oak reception counter, smiling, exposing straight white teeth. This close, he could see a there was indeed a light dusting of freckles on her nose, visible even through the pink blush staining her cheeks. Her smile made his blood surge, but it was her big brown eyes, the color of dark topaz, that really knocked him for a loop all over again.

He said the first thing that popped into his head. "What's up with your dog?"

Her blush deepened. "Oh, I am so sorry. He's a little…wild." She bit her lip and glanced toward the smudged window. "I'll be sure and clean up his paw and nose marks." Her voice was distinctive—melodious and sexy at the same time.

"Don't worry about it. Maybe he needs some obedience training," Connor offered. "A training collar might help."

She widened her eyes. "You mean a choke collar?" she said, horror studding every syllable. "That would hurt him."

"A car nailing him would hurt more. Luckily, there's no traffic in Oak Valley, or he might have been hit."

She pressed her lips into a fine line. "I have my own ways of training my dog—"

"Ways that work?"

She snapped her mouth closed and glared. "My dog isn't the issue here." She stepped forward and grudgingly offered her hand. "You must be Dr. Forbes." She sounded as if she thought he'd morphed into Dr. Frankenstein.

He took the proffered hand and shook it, liking how smooth and warm and small it felt in his, how its heat spread instantly into his body. "Uh, yes. Yes I am." He tilted his head sideways and reluctantly released her, noticing her light floral scent in the air, wishing he could lean in close and sniff. He *really* hoped she wasn't a patient. It would be unethical to have the sorts of thoughts he was having if he was supposed to treat her. "And you are?"

"Sunny Williams." She scanned the area, her tight look fading a bit. "I can't tell you how much I've looked forward to coming here, Dr. Forbes. I fully believe my holistic approach to healing will add a wonderful new dimension to your practice."

He pulled in his chin, surprised by not only how fitting her name was, but also that he had absolutely no idea what she was talking about. "Holistic healing? You mean all of that ridiculous, New Age mumbo jumbo?"

She bristled again. "It's not mumbo jumbo," she replied, her eyes sparking. "I deal in massage therapy, yoga and aromatherapy."

"And it will add a new dimension to *my* practice?" He laughed under his breath, shaking his head. "You've got the wrong guy." He didn't believe in that kind of garbage. Science was the backbone of his medical practice, not the touchy-feely theories that were making the rounds these days.

She pursed her glossy lips and frowned, creating appealing little lines between her dark blond eyebrows. "I don't think so." She put her tote bag on the floor and raised one brow. "You're Connor Forbes, right?"

He widened his stance, crossing his arms over his chest. "Yes, I am, but I don't know who *you* are."

Mild panic rose in her eyes; then, her face cleared and she grinned. "Oh, that rascal."

"Who are you talking about?"

"Why, your father, of course." She pushed her hair behind her ear and gave him a funny look. "Who else?"

Connor stared at her, the bottom falling out of his stomach. "My father?"

Nodding, she said, "He met my parents at a marriage counseling workshop, found out I was looking to make a new start, and he invited me to come here and set up shop next door." She gestured to the empty storefront next to his. "I guess we got off on the wrong foot." She extended her hand again. "I'm Sunny Williams, your new partner."

His partner?

Connor stared at her hand, trying to ignore how much he wanted to touch her again. He shoved his glasses back on. Raw anger began to bubble inside of him, along with a burning question he was damn sure going to find the answer to.

What in the heck was his dad up to?

Sunny withdrew her hand when the doctor didn't shake it. She took a little breath to calm her racing heart, attributing her breathlessness to the fact that Rufus had been his usual naughty self this morning, leading her on a wild goose chase before she'd caught him. To make matters worse, he'd been naughty in front of her new partner, mortifying her in the process. It didn't help at all that her new partner had never heard of her.

Struggling for calm, she noticed again that Dr. Forbes was one darn good-looking man, even with that stunned I-didn't-know-I-had-a-partner expression on his hand-some face. His deep green eyes, disheveled, dark brown hair and tall, muscular body made him look like her male fantasy come to life. She even liked his glasses, which gave him a scholarly air, and his rumpled tan cor-duroy trousers and light blue button-down cotton shirt looked appealing on him.

Then he'd opened his mouth. Choke collar! Ridicu-lous, New Age mumbo jumbo indeed!

But she'd have to set aside her dislike for the sake of her career goals. Oak Valley was her fresh start, a new chance to make a go of it with her holistic therapy practice. She'd failed in San Francisco. A lot. She wouldn't—couldn't—fail again. Seeing the disappointment in her parents' eyes—again—after their own wild success would be too much to bear.

Besides, until she'd encountered the disagreeable doctor, she'd felt nothing but positive vibes from Oak Valley. This *had* to be the place. Her thirtieth birthday was coming up fast. And Robbie was already married. She needed an anchor, and she hoped she'd find one here in Oak Valley.

The doctor finally spoke. "Look, I don't know what kind of arrangement you made with my father, but I'm not in the market for a partner. Especially not one into holistic healing." He rolled his eyes. "What was he thinking, anyway?"

She clenched her jaw, her hopes sliding; then she shoved her chin in the air, refusing to let this man mess up her dream. "He was looking to add a fresh dimension to this practice, which it looks like you need." She crossed her arms over her chest and drilled him with a hard look. "What have you got against what I do?"

He pierced her with his gaze. "What I do is based on science, period. Anything else is of no use to me."

She stepped forward, annoyed by his negative, judgmental attitude. She pointed at him. "So let me get this straight. You think what I do is totally useless?"

He nodded without hesitation. "Pretty much."

She told herself she shouldn't be surprised. She'd known attitudes would be different outside of San Francisco. But she'd come here with Dr. Brady Forbes's blessing and hadn't expected to run into such opposition from his son.

Even though she wanted to scream at the stubborn doctor, she tried to focus on the positive. She managed a tight little smile. "Well, then I guess I'll just have to change your mind, won't I?"

He didn't smile back. "I'm afraid that's a waste of time, Ms. Williams," he said, taking off his glasses. "I have no intention of having you, or anybody else, as my partner. I'm sorry you came all this way to find that out, but I'm the Dr. Forbes in charge now, not my father, and I wasn't in on this deal. I don't feel obligated to honor it."

Sunny stared at him, wishing he didn't attract her so much on the outside when, on the inside, where it really mattered, he was a walking billboard for the uptight, repressed and uninformed.

She switched gears to the really bad news. Her dream of starting over and finally succeeding in business in this wonderful little town was suddenly in jeopardy.

This infuriating man was refusing to work with her. He probably didn't have a clue about working with anyone but himself, about nurturing a relationship, business or otherwise.

She remembered something his father had told her, and recalled the words she'd seen painted on the window of this office when she'd pulled Rufus off the glass. A thought occurred to her. She gazed speculatively at the doctor, grimly holding her frustration at bay in favor of finding a way to make this work. She needed this job, needed to live in this town and be married by her thirtieth birthday, needed to succeed. "So are you the new Mr. Commitment?"

He rolled his eyes and nodded, then let out a disgusted sound. "Yeah."

She raised a brow, pretty sure she was now coming at this problem from the right angle. "You don't sound too happy about that."

"I'm a medical doctor, not a relationship counselor."

"So you don't think you're qualified? Is that it?" she pressed, leaning closer, catching a vague whiff of his clean, soapy scent. Her breath caught in her throat.

He scowled at her. "What's with all the questions?"

"Hear me out," she said, holding out a hand. "You don't think you're qualified to be a relationship counselor, right?"

He lifted a broad shoulder. "I guess you could say that. I'm the last person who should be helping people mend their relationships." Turning away, he opened a fat file on the counter. "My track record stinks," he muttered under his breath.

Sunny assumed he was talking about his relationships. No surprise there. The man appeared to have the warmth of a rock and not a compassionate bone in his body. Luckily, she found that information about his past fascinating—and useful, exactly the ammunition she needed.

Unable to corral her need to understand her adversary, she asked, "Why are you here if you're so unqualified to be Mr. Commitment? Why not take a job somewhere else?"

He swung his darkening gaze her way. "Not that it's any of your business, but I agreed to come home and take over for my dad years ago, back when Mr. Commitment didn't exist. I had no idea that I'd be required to hold my patients' hands regarding their relationship issues. Believe me, if I'd had any idea, I never would have agreed."

"Then you need me."

He crossed his arms across his broad chest again. "Oh, really?" he said, his voice rife with amusement.

She gave a quick nod, unwilling to let his bad attitude back her down. "Really. I have a knack for helping people with problems. Maybe we should make a deal— my relationship expertise in exchange for a partnership."

He let out a heavy breath and abruptly flipped the file on the counter closed. "No deal, Ms. Williams. I don't need help with Mr. Commitment that badly." He straightened and inclined his head. "Now if you'll excuse me, I have a patient in a few minutes." With that, he exited the waiting room through a door in back of the counter, leaving Sunny alone.

And desperate. She'd been counting on this job to prove to herself, and to her parents, that she could make a success doing what she loved. Not to mention that she was dead broke. She needed this job for so many reasons, and she really wanted to stay in Oak Valley and settle down.

The need for the commitment and stability she'd never had growing up still burned inside of her like a smoldering fire, impossible to put out or ignore.

Besides, a pact was a pact.

But one man had torn up her dreams with his highly questionable bedside manner—what a grump!—and my-way-or-the-highway beliefs about healing. Uptight Connor Forbes claimed he didn't have any use for a partner.

A tight knot formed in her chest. She had to think of a way to change his mind.

Maybe a cup of herbal tea and a bagel were what she needed to maintain an even keel during this unexpected, upsetting crisis. It was a cool morning, even though the sun was shining. Rufus would be fine if she put him in the van for an hour or so, especially since she'd parked in the shade.

With a sigh, she picked up her bag and headed out the door, hoping Oak Valley had a restaurant open for breakfast. She simply needed time to figure out how to deal with Doctor Disagreeable's rejection.

She laughed humorlessly under her breath, feeling the fool. Her reliable instincts told her there wasn't enough herbal tea in the world to help her change the stubborn, absolutely annoying man's mind.

Talk about an awkward situation, Connor thought. Gorgeous female massage therapist/yoga instructor unexpectedly shows up at his father's behest, expecting to be Connor's partner, nosing her way into his business. He might want to be her partner in other things—she'd smelled, and looked, really good—and a little feminine companionship sounded great.

But his business partner? No way. Even though he wasn't the type of guy who wanted to make a pretty girl sad, he'd find a way to live with that.

He shook his head and sat down behind his oak desk. Damn his father for arranging something so outrageous without his approval. It was bad enough Dad was demanding that Connor take the dubious title of Mr. Commitment. Now he was making business deals with medically unqualified people. What was the old guy thinking?

Connor shoved his reading glasses in his lab coat pocket and pushed his irritation with his dad aside in favor of the controlled, professional attitude he always strived for when he was with patients. He proceeded with his day and saw two patients, Margery Leventhal, who had vague stomach complaints that turned out to be simple gas, and Jeb Hornsby, whose gout was acting up.

Connor then took his usual morning break and strolled down the boardwalk to Luella's Diner for a doughnut and coffee. On the way, he lifted a hand to Lester Parsons and Ozzie Peterson, two retirees who were sitting at their usual morning spot on a bench in front of Jeremiah's Barber Shop across the street. He smiled at Abigail McNeil, out walking her basset hound, and greeted Frank Osbourne, the local contractor, who was loading his pickup with building supplies outside Truman's Hardware Store.

Connor shook his head. A man couldn't burp in Oak Valley without the whole town knowing it. After living in a big city like Seattle, he'd expected to feel stifled here, and that had proven true. He liked the people of Oak Valley well enough, but everyone had always bugged him to loosen up. If things worked out the way he'd planned, he wouldn't have to stay here forever.

A few minutes later, Connor stepped into Luella's, enjoying the usual aroma of sizzling bacon, fresh brewed coffee and fried doughnuts. Luella's place had looked the same since Connor was a kid and his parents had brought him and his siblings here for Sunday breakfast. The quaint eatery boasted rustic tables and booths with high backs, white paper placemats, red-and-white checked curtains and a long counter with worn wooden stools.

As she did every day, Luella's daughter, Mary-Jean, waved to him from the kitchen, visible through the cutout wall behind the counter. He smiled halfway and waved back. She was always so friendly to him. For the life of him, he couldn't figure out why—he had said only a handful of words to her.

He noticed Steve McCarthy, an old high school classmate, sitting in a back booth, enjoying a cup of coffee with his sister, Julie, who'd married Bud Whitesell, the owner of the local garage. Connor waved at them and then went to sit in the third booth from the door, his usual spot. He looked forward to a cup of hot coffee and a sinfully fattening doughnut. He'd think about anything but Sunny Williams.

Just as that idea ran through his brain, he saw the subject of his thoughts sitting in *his* booth, a cup of tea and a half-eaten bagel in front of her, talking animatedly to, of all people, his own sister, Jennifer.

He raised his brows. Sunny had certainly made friends quickly. Obviously, she was the outgoing, friendly type. She would probably fit in with his sociable family perfectly. He gritted his teeth.

Despite the fact that he was irritated she was in his booth, he couldn't help but appreciate her beautiful skin, delicate bone structure and flashing brown eyes all over again. And her shiny pink lips, pulled into a broad, appealing smile, exposing straight, white teeth, made his insides burn.

He didn't want his insides burning, knew from experience what kind of failure that always brought about, despite his need to socialize with someone of the female persuasion who wasn't his mother or his sister. He clenched his jaw tighter, ready to cut out.

Jenny noticed him, smiled and spoke up. "Hey, Connor, have you met Sunny?" She turned to Sunny and gestured to Connor. "This is my brother, Connor."

Sunny looked up and her smile faded. "Oh, we've already met."

He inclined his head. "Yes, we have, haven't we?"

Jenny frowned and looked at Sunny. "Didn't you say you just arrived in town?"

"I did." Sunny took a sip of tea. "I stopped by your brother's office first thing." She put her tea down, smiled and drilled him with her amber-shaded gaze. "We had business, didn't we, Dr. Forbes?"

He nodded, betting she was going to go into how he'd turned down her bid to be his partner to Jenny, whose mission in life was to take over.

Jennifer looked at him, one blond brow raised. "What kind of business, Connor?" She glanced back at Sunny. "You're not sick, are you?"

Sunny shook her head. "No, I'm not."

"Then what…?" Jenny asked, looking back and forth between them.

To her credit, Sunny remained silent, her gaze now on her teacup, when she could have busted him to his sister. He forced out a breath. He might as well come clean. Jenny would ferret out the truth eventually, and would definitely hear about it from their dad. Besides, he'd done the right thing. Sunny's treatment methods had no place in his world. She was a temptation he wanted to avoid. No way was he changing his mind.

Connor sat down next to Jenny. "Dad brought Sunny here to be my partner. I vetoed the idea," he said, dumping out the whole story in a few words. He braced himself, waiting for Jenny's outrage.

She gasped and widened her eyes. "You did what?" she said, delivering the expected reaction right on cue. She was so predictable, even to someone like him, who, according to his second-to-last girlfriend, was horribly left-brained and didn't clue into people's personalities very well.

"I said no," he reiterated, wanting this whole thing over. "End of story."

"But why?" Jenny asked, her voice rife with amazed puzzlement. "Sunny's just what you need, brother."

He ignored the *need* Sunny could help him with and shook his head. "I know what I need, and she's not it."

He gazed at Sunny. "It's nothing personal. I just don't want a partner."

Sunny stared back, nodding. "Oh, so when you said that everything you do is based on science, and anything else is of no use to you, you didn't mean for me to take it personally?" She lobbed him a sweet-edged smile. "I would hate to misunderstand you, Dr. Forbes."

"Connor!" Jenny said, her hazel eyes full of sisterly horror. "Tell me you didn't say that."

Both women stared at him; if looks could kill, he'd be keeling over dead. What was the big deal? "Look, I based my decision on concrete, practical reasoning," he said, explaining his rationale. "I simply meant that my practice is based on science, not massage or yoga, and that Sunny and I wouldn't be compatible working partners. Dad arranged this without my knowledge and since I'm in charge now, I felt I had the right to make that decision."

They were silent for a few moments, and then Jenny gave a long-suffering sigh and skewered him with a hard gaze. "You're so full of it, Connor. The truth is, you're a stick-in-the-mud from way back. The thought of doing something differently, of straying one millimeter from your moldy science textbooks and boring medical journals scares the pants off of you."

He mentally rolled his eyes. His family had been trying to loosen him up for years, Jenny especially. She just didn't understand that he was his own man and was nothing like her or anyone else in his family.

While he sat there wondering why he needed to explain something so simple, Sunny reached over and touched his forearm, sending sparks racing up his arm. She chimed in with, "Don't worry, Dr. Forbes. I'm sure you look very, very good with no pants."

Jenny and Sunny laughed and Connor raised his brows at Sunny. Wow. She was something, able to fling the horse manure right back at him. Oddly, he liked that.

So what? He might appreciate her spunk, but he wasn't about to let her know it, or let it matter. She stared back, a becoming blush spreading across her cheeks. Then her eyes popped wide and she jerked her hand back, knocking Jenny's orange juice over.

Right onto his lap.

He let out a colorful oath. Sunny jumped up and clapped a hand over her mouth. "Oh, oh, I'm so sorry." She picked up a napkin, obviously intending to blot up the mess.

She stopped, her hand holding the napkin hovering over his juice-saturated lap. "Uh, well…" She blushed and waved the napkin. "I…guess you better take care of that." She shoved the napkin at him. "I'm so sorry. I'm not usually the clumsy sort."

He took the napkin, her blush conjuring up all kinds of thoughts he shouldn't be having, and dabbed at his lap. "Yeah, I'll bet." He heard a snorting sound and swung his gaze to Jenny, who was holding a hand over her mouth, trying to keep her laugh contained and doing a bad job of it.

Sunny sat down, her cheeks blazing pink, her pretty

brown eyes reflecting her obvious embarrassment. Man, her gorgeous face would be tough to forget.

But he would. He didn't need a partner and he certainly didn't need to fail at another relationship, although a no-strings-attached date sounded good…

Before the conversation started up again, Julie approached the table, her first pregnancy just beginning to show. "Uh, Connor, could I talk to you for a moment?"

He nodded, hiding his wet lap with his napkin. "Sure, Julie, what's up? The baby okay?"

"Yeah, he's just fine," she said, rubbing a hand over her burgeoning belly. "I was needing to talk to Mr. Commitment."

Oh, man. Not that. "Uh, well, Julie—"

"The thing is, Bud works all day, sometimes late, and when he comes home, all he wants to do is crash in front of the TV, watching sports. I'm kind of lonely, Doc. What do you suggest?"

He sat and thought for a moment, and incredibly, the answer to her problem was easy to figure out. "That sounds like nothing a good book wouldn't solve, Julie."

She stared at him, her chin pulled in. "You think?"

"I'm sure of it," he said, patting her hand. "Reading will keep you entertained for hours." Maybe this Mr. Commitment stuff wouldn't be so hard after all.

She wandered off, shaking her head.

When he looked at Jenny and Sunny, both were sporting dropped jaws and wide eyes. "What?" he asked.

Jenny gave him a long-suffering look and said, "You're clueless and hopeless." She then stood and gestured with a crook of her hand for Sunny to follow. "Come on, Sunny. My brother isn't the only one with some say-so around here." She gave him a saccharine smile. "Thanks for picking up the tab."

Connor stood and Sunny slid out of the booth, smiling, though it seemed forced. "Thanks for everything, Dr. Forbes."

Meaning, thanks for *nothing*. He had to give her credit. She obviously had a knack for holding her own. One more thing to like. One more reason to forget her.

Jenny called Sunny from the door of the diner. Sunny gave him a sheepish look, her plump bottom lip clamped between her teeth. "I gotta go." She glanced down at his lap. "Do, uh, you have that taken care of?" She snapped her gaze back up, her face coloring again. "The juice spill, I mean."

Seeing her so flustered forced a smile. "It's fine, nothing that won't dry."

She nodded, moving away. "Oh, good." She waved. "Bye."

He was left standing next to the booth alone, Sunny's floral scent belatedly washing over him after she'd walked by. Despite the coolness of the spilled juice, heat flared down low.

He was tempted to turn around and watch her walk away so he could enjoy the sight of her slim but curvy hips moving beneath her skirt and her toned calves flexing as she walked.

Instead, he sat and took a swig of strong, hot coffee, an irritating helplessness washing over him. Just his damn luck Sunny seemed like just the woman to put an end to his desire for some casual female companionship.

Just as bad, Sunny had met Jenny. His younger sister was as tenacious as a mule when she felt someone had been treated unfairly.

Who would have guessed that Sunny would be the type of gal who would meet a total stranger and strike up a sudden friendship, all in the space of an hour? More than likely, she *would* be able to help him with Mr. Commitment. She clearly had an outgoing, friendly, approachable personality, just like Jenny.

Bad combination, those two. Jenny, the fired-up defender of the innocent working with Sunny, her name the perfect description of her personality. Even when she'd slammed him, it had come out in a way that had amused everybody, even him. And no other woman had looked so good after spilling juice all over him.

Yeah, Sunny was appealing in so many ways, making her dangerous. And he had a sneaking suspicion that with Jenny and Sunny working together, the situation would more than likely do what he hated—spin out of his control and out of the realm of practicality.

And right into the realm of intense physical—and, more dangerously, emotional—attraction.

And that was the last place he would ever let himself go.

Chapter Two

Connor pushed his dark thoughts aside, ignored his wet, orange juice–saturated lap, chomped on his doughnut and drank his coffee. He reiterated to himself why he'd made the right decision, the practical one for his practice.

Just as he finished the doughnut, Steve approached his booth. "Hey, Doc. How you doing?"

Connor inclined his head. "All right." He and Steve had gone through school together and had shared an interest in science. Steve had combined his interest in the scientific world with his love of animals and had become a veterinarian.

Steve smiled. "Saw your sister here a few minutes ago."

Connor nodded and took a sip of coffee. "That was her."

"Who was that gorgeous gal with her?" Steve asked,

his brown eyes alight with interest. "Haven't seen her around before."

Connor gave Steve a hard glance. "Sunny Williams," he said, not particularly hot on going into details. The whole town knew Steve was in the market for a wife.

Steve plunked down across from him. "Is she living in Oak Valley, or just visiting?"

"Just visiting." Connor was pretty sure Sunny would leave now that she didn't have a job. He had to admit, as an appreciative, red-blooded male, part of him was a bit disappointed a gorgeous woman like Sunny wasn't going to be hanging around.

"Too bad," Steve said, shaking his head. "Wouldn't mind getting to know her."

Surprisingly, the thought of Steve *getting to know* Sunny bothered Connor. Irritated that he was bothered at all, he finished his coffee, stood and reached for the tab. "Don't think you'll have the chance, bud. She won't be here for long."

He said goodbye, hiding his splotched pants as best he could, then paid the bill at the front counter and left. As he walked up the boardwalk, the late morning sun warm on his back, he told himself he'd done the right thing, even though his dad would probably come unglued. That couldn't be helped. Despite his father's inevitable anger and disappointment, Connor's decision would stand.

Confident he'd done the right thing, he walked back to his office. When he arrived, his next patient, ten-year-old Danny Jones, was waiting. Connor quickly donned his lab coat to hide his damp clothes, then tended to Danny.

Danny had recently broken his arm playing baseball, and Connor wanted to make sure the healing process was on track. Danny's parents had been killed in a car accident two years ago, and he'd come to Oak Valley to live with his widowed grandmother, Edith Largo, a long-time resident. Connor had spent a lot of time with Danny, trying to fill in here and there to give Edith a break and a guy for the kid to play ball with.

Pleased by Danny's rate of recovery, Connor walked him to the waiting room, noting his dad, the elder Dr. Forbes, sat in the waiting room, shooting the breeze with June and Edith.

Damn. Obviously Jenny and Sunny had called in the cavalry. His dad looked at him expectantly. Connor clenched his hands.

Smiling to cover up the tension suddenly roiling around the room, Connor conferred with Edith. He then made an appointment in two weeks for Danny's cast to be removed and walked him and Edith to the door.

When they were gone, his dad stood, his perennial red baseball cap in his hand. "I expected you'd have a special visitor by now."

Connor paused, gathering his patience together, then crossed his arms over his chest. "So I suppose Sunny and Jenny came to see you."

His dad looked puzzled. "No. But does that mean Sunny's here? Have you had a chance to meet?"

Major surprise. So the threatening twosome hadn't

gone running to his dad as he'd assumed. Score one small point for Sunny. "Sunny came here, and then I saw her and Jenny at Luella's half an hour ago, but I don't know where they went after that."

June piped in. "She and Jenny came by, got Sunny's dog out of her van and took him for a walk."

His dad stepped forward, his hazel eyes questioning. "I expected that she'd be next door getting organized. Is she coming back later?"

"No, because I have no intention of being her partner. The deal is off." He stared at his dad, scowling. "Really, Dad, you should have consulted me before you brought her on. You know how I feel about alternative medicine."

His dad's eyes hardened. "Yes, I do, which is one of the reasons I asked her to come here." His dad pointed at him. "You need an overhaul, my boy."

He stared at his dad, minutely shaking his head. Connor had become a doctor to prove to his dad that they shared a unique connection. But catering to the desire to forge a bond with his father wasn't going to happen this time. His dad had stepped over the line.

He gave his dad a stony look and said, "Is there anything else?"

His dad stepped up to the counter and pounded his fist on it. "Dammit, Connor, you're not going to do your usual number and just walk away when things get sticky. I expect you to go along with this."

Connor gritted his teeth, but before he could say "Forget it," his dad continued. "And I'll throw this out as bait. Your mother is driving me crazy at home now that I'm retired. I love her, but I'm going nuts with all of her honey-do's. If you do this for me and allow Sunny to be your partner for say…a three-month trial period, I'll reconsider full-time retirement after that."

Connor raised his brows. He had to give the old man some credit. He'd thrown out a tempting deal, especially since what Connor really wanted to do—pursue a career in medical research and leave Oak Valley behind—would be that much easier to accomplish if his dad was around to help out.

Granted, he hadn't figured out how he could be a medical researcher and still fulfill his long-ago promise to his parents to permanently take over for his dad in exchange for them putting him through med school. He hadn't even told them about his dream of a different career.

He let out a heavy breath. Okay, he'd work on that and come up with something. Maybe he'd even be able to convince his dad to go back to being Mr. Commitment, too. One more reason to take him up on the deal.

True, Connor would have to put up with Sunny's hokey massage business and yoga. He could take that for three months, couldn't he?

Maybe as his working partner. But as a sexy, tempting woman he'd have to keep his hands off of? He swallowed. Suddenly, three months seemed like a lifetime.

He ignored that thought. "You've got yourself a deal."

His dad smiled. "I knew you'd see reason. I promise you won't regret your decision. Sunny is a wonderful, charming woman who will be a terrific addition to this office." He moved toward the door. "Junie tells me you don't have another patient for over an hour. Instead of stuffing your nose in some medical journal, why don't you go find Sunny and give her the good news?" He waved, plopped his hat on his head and walked out.

Connor stared at the door and then rubbed his neck, trying to relieve the perpetual crick there. Suddenly, a massage by the delectable Miss Sunshine sounded pretty good.

He swung around, tightening his jaw. She was getting to him already.

Too bad. He'd agreed to the deal. He'd just have to be sure to stick to his vow to keep his thoughts where they belonged—anywhere but on beautiful Sunny Williams. He wasn't going to be tempted into certain romantic failure again.

Get real, Forbes. He had a bad feeling that keeping his mind off of brown-eyed Sunny wasn't going to be easy. She turned him on in a major way and seemed pretty nice, too, even when she was spitting fire.

Damn, he hoped he wouldn't regret agreeing to his dad's harebrained deal.

Sunny sat on a quaint, wrought-iron bench in the park, waiting for Rufus to come back with the tennis ball she'd thrown. She was determined to chill out and enjoy the sunny, peaceful morning and picturesque, grassy little park, located on the edge of town, while she figured out what to do next. Jenny had left to pick up her daughter at her parents' house with a promise not to talk to her dad, leaving Sunny alone with her thoughts.

Despite her efforts to calm down and simply enjoy her surroundings, frustratingly dire thoughts—centering around one stubborn, irritating doctor—swamped her.

After so many business and romantic flops, she'd been so excited about moving here, making a new start and proving to herself that she wasn't a total failure. This might be her last chance to fulfill her pact with Robbie and secure the commitment they'd craved as footloose best friends being raised in a commune.

Commitment. Inevitably, her thoughts swung to her parents. Sunny had always felt vulnerable since her parents had never married, worried that they didn't love each other enough to make it official, that they would split up. It hadn't helped that they had separated three times during her childhood. Even though she'd never suspected her parents had been unfaithful, because of their upsetting separations, when she was ten, she swore that she would eventually find a good man, fall in love and commit, creating the rooted environment that had always been missing in her life.

That vow had been cemented in stone when she and Robbie had made their promise to marry each other, fueled by her need for security and stability, for a comforting anchor, a need that lived on inside of her to this day.

Consequently, she'd been thrilled when the elder Dr. Forbes had made her the offer to come to Oak Valley. Build a new business. Find the ideal, steadfast man to commit to, fulfill the pact and, hopefully, heal the wound Robbie had created by marrying someone else. Create a secure, small-town life. It all had seemed so wonderfully picture-perfect.

Until this morning. Until Connor Forbes had entered the picture and put an ugly blotch on what was to have been her perfect life.

Rufus brought the ball back, wagging his spotted tail. He dropped it and she threw it again. He ran off, chasing the thing down. The goofy dog would play this game forever if she let him.

Her thoughts careened back to her problems. So, she'd run into one big, handsome, annoying roadblock. How could she prove to him that what she did had worth—admittedly not as a total replacement for his brand of traditional medicine, but as a complement? She'd always subscribed to the notion, Heal the Heart, Heal the Body," believing that maintaining and encouraging a peaceful inner self would help foster a healthy outer self, the body. How in the world was she going to convince Connor to reconsider, to give her methods a chance to fill in the blanks his methods often left?

Before she could answer her own question, a male voice spoke from behind her. "Your dog's a horse."

Her tummy flip-flopped. Taking a deep breath, she turned and saw Connor standing in back of her, his bulging arms folded across his broad chest. His dark hair glinted in the sun like warm chocolate and his green eyes looked like dark emeralds. A ripple of feminine awareness skated up her spine. Why did he look so darned good, his masculine appeal so blatantly obvious?

Cutting off her mental list of his positive traits, she forced herself to remember how he'd heartlessly cut her loose. Her hands clenched, she turned back and watched Rufus bound clumsily back with his beloved tennis ball in his mouth. "Great Dane. Definitely a dog."

Rufus spotted Connor and immediately dropped the ball, woofed and ran over to him, his tail swinging back and forth like a giant whip.

Obviously unintimidated by Rufus's size, Connor smiled and said, "Hey, big guy," holding out his hand so Rufus could sniff it. Then Connor began to gently pet the big lug. Rufus whined, then proceeded to lie down and roll onto his back. Connor obliged him and squatted and rubbed the dog's good-sized belly, grudgingly scoring major points in Sunny's book.

Connor looked up and smiled. "He's just a big baby, isn't he?"

She nodded, chuckling despite her negative mood. "You've got that right. He's huge, but doesn't have a mean bone in his body. Right, Rufus?"

Rufus didn't acknowledge her, just lay there, his legs splayed, soaking up his first tummy rub of the day. Connor undoubtedly had no idea that he'd made a friend for life. Rufus wasn't nearly picky enough about whom he associated with.

A long silence stretched out, and Sunny's curiosity got the best of her. "So, why are you here? You made it pretty clear you wanted nothing to do with me. Need another glass of juice spilled on you?"

Connor rose and ran a hand through his hair. He

moved toward her, what looked like forced contrition showing in his eyes. "Sorry about what I said. I don't always express myself very well."

She hoisted up a brow. "Oh, I think you got your point across pretty well."

He sat down next to her and his soapy, male scent washed over her, raising her awareness level a notch.

"My whole family tells me I'm tactless," he said, seemingly without regret. "I prefer to call it being refreshingly direct."

She pulled in her chin and said, "Refreshing?" She laughed under her breath and rolled her eyes. "Yeah, right. That's a good one."

"Why don't you tell me how you really feel," he said, sarcasm dripping from every word.

"Okay," she said, taking him up on his offer even though she was sure he wasn't really interested in her feelings. "Actually, I'd like to stomp on your head. You've ruined my plans." She took the ball from Rufus and hurled it across the grass. "I was sitting here trying to figure out how to change such a stubborn, grouchy man's mind."

"Don't hold back, now."

She stared at him. "Trust me. I won't."

"I can see that," he said dryly. "Actually, grumpiness aside, you have a good plan, trying to change my mind. Very practical."

"And are you always practical, Dr. Forbes? You strike me as the type who tries to be sensible at all times." Sensible and totally repressed: boy, did he need to loosen up.

"I try to be." He angled his body toward her and rested his left elbow on the back of the bench, bringing himself slightly closer. He pierced her with his eyes. "Is that bad?"

She shifted on the hard bench again and fiddled with the ends of her hair, uneasy with his nearness and how aware she was of his heat and scent. What was wrong with her, letting his physical appeal get to her? She didn't even like the man. "Uh, well, not always, although sometimes it's better to go with your gut instincts rather than what's practical. A person's inner voice is important, don't you think?"

He inclined his head. "I guess. It's been proven that instincts have helped man survive for thousands of years."

She wanted to snort. Of course, he'd twisted her beliefs around so that they reeked of scientific fact rather than what he simply knew, deep down inside. He was obviously so out of touch with himself.

Ignoring how much she'd like to help him with that particular problem—boy, would she like to get a hold of his broad, well-muscled shoulders and work all of his tense, uptightness right out of his body—she focused instead on the question that was still gnawing at her.

"So, why did you come find me?" she asked, trying to sound casual. "I figured our business was finished."

Rufus ran up, flopped down next to Connor and gazed up adoringly at him. Connor obliged and patted his head. "I've reconsidered." He turned and held out his hand, his eyes boring into hers. "How about you shake hands with your new partner?"

Sunny widened her eyes, taken totally off guard by his unexpected offer. She automatically put her hand in his warm grip, liking the way his large hand engulfed hers. "You've changed your mind?" she asked, doubt spilling over. She quickly pulled free of his compelling touch to stay in control.

He nodded and then quickly looked away, his gaze focused across the park. "I guess I have."

His inability to meet her eyes set off alarms in her head. "Why?"

"Change of heart," he said, casually—too casually— lifting one broad shoulder.

She stared at him, her reliable intuition kicking into gear. She frowned slightly. "Really? An hour ago you were very clear about what you thought about partnering with me, and it wasn't good." She narrowed her gaze. "What's going on?"

He shook his head. "I guess I can't fool you." He inclined his head. "All right, I'll come clean. My dad changed my mind."

She gave a humorless laugh, doing a bad job of covering up the ache building inside of her. "Ah, I should have known your change of heart was really just your father forcing you to honor the deal." She pressed her lips together and glared at him. "So what did he offer you to cooperate?"

"He offered to come out of retirement part-time."

She pulled her brows together. "Okay. But how does that help you, except for cutting down on your work load?"

"I want to get into medical research. That'll be easier to do if he's helping me out. He also offered a trial period. Of three months."

She glared at him. "The heart of the matter at last. You're probably thinking you'll just bide your time for three months, then get rid of me, right?"

His stony silence gave her the answer.

With anger building in her—she felt like stomping on his head again—she quickly rose and began pacing before he could reply. "So you're only doing this because of your dad's offer rather than because of some newfound respect for what I do, right?"

He shrugged. "Hey, I have an agenda, just like you do. This will help me achieve it."

Well, she had to give him credit for being honest, but that was as generous as she'd be. His attitude cut deep. Her wounded pride reared up, along with a healthy dose of her usual idealism. Partnering with a man with no respect for her methods would be wrong—and counterproductive. She'd be working under a cloud of contempt that would surely overwhelm her eventually. No, she couldn't—wouldn't—work under those uncertain, pride-shredding circumstances, no matter how desperate she was to finally settle into a successful career.

She stared at him. "Thanks for the offer, but no thanks. You have no respect for what I do, no appreciation for any medical treatment not based in your kind of science. You only want to use me to help you further your own goals. I don't think you're the partner *I'm* looking for." She picked up Rufus's leash and hooked it to his collar, then gave a stunned-looking Connor a sweet, totally fake smile. "Goodbye."

Connor stood and put a hand on her arm. "Sunny, wait—"

Rufus's hysterical barking cut him off. Before Sunny could react, Rufus started running in circles while he barked at a squirrel running up the trunk of a nearby tree. His leash wrapped around Connor's legs and then Sunny's, round and round, pulling them closer and closer together.

"Rufus, stop!" she hollered. But it was too late to get the leash off her wrist and Rufus was too strong and too rambunctious. She and Connor were quickly bound together by the tangled leash, his big body pressed intimately up against hers.

Rufus quit barking and the leash went slack. The silly dog whined, looking everywhere for that darn squirrel.

Doing nothing to extricate himself, Connor looked down at Sunny, his darkening gaze zeroing in on her, and said, "Your dog needs a firmer hand."

Sunny stared up at him, stunned into inaction, heat building inside, almost drowning in his gorgeous green eyes. She could only nod, wishing in some far, foolish corner of her brain that he would kiss her.

Oh, my stars! He must have had the same idea. A moment later, he lowered his head, bringing his hands to her shoulders and his lips to within inches of hers. "Although I guess there are some advantages to having a naughty dog, right?" He moved closer still, his breath washing over her, his male heat searing her. Her heart raced and her breath stalled in her throat. He dropped his head—

Rufus yanked on the leash, hard, barking frantically again. In an instant, she and Connor went from almost kissing to falling over like a giant, leash-wrapped felled tree. Sunny squealed and Connor let out a hearty "Whoa!"

Fortunately for Sunny, but not for Connor, he landed on the bottom with an *oof,* cushioning her fall. She came to rest on top of him, her legs entangled with his, her body plastered from head to toe against him. His masculine, spicy scent surrounded her, warming her from the inside out.

Bad reaction. She struggled to get free, wiggling and flailing, letting out a few unladylike grunts, one thought front and center in her mind:

He'd almost kissed her!

Worse yet, she'd been well past the brink of letting him. Luckily, Rufus's antics had stopped that in the nick of time. Connor wasn't the man she was looking for. She had no business kissing him.

She needed to get away. She tried to stand, but her lower legs were still tangled in the leash. Muttering dark thoughts, she rolled off Connor to the ground, her feet still bound to his.

"Rufus, you big, stupid mutt, come here!" she said, pulling on his leash. Rufus whined and meekly obeyed. Sunny quickly unhooked his leash from his collar, then unwrapped it from their legs, still holding him with one hand.

As soon as she could, she stood, brushing herself off with one hand, hoping her blush had faded. She re-hooked Rufus's leash, took a deep breath and looked at Connor, who'd stood, too.

"I'll be going now," she said to Connor in as normal a voice as possible, unable to meet his probing gaze. "I'm sure you'll be able to explain why I didn't accept your little deal to your father."

With that, she started walking, her head held high, Rufus trotting along at her side. She softened her earlier harsh words with a stroke to the dog's big head. Connor didn't stop her this time, and she was glad. He flustered and confused her and she hated that. She might be broke, but she still had her pride, despite their little near kiss.

And Connor Forbes was right where he wanted to be before his dad stepped in.

On his own.

His runaway heartbeat was thundering in his ears as Connor watched Sunny walk away, noting with lots of male appreciation how her blond hair looked like white gold glowing in the sun. He wished she'd come back here and tangle herself up with him again. He'd come so close to kissing her, to letting his desire run its course. He was sure he would never forget the feel of her soft, curvy body moving around on top of him…

He snorted, jerking his thoughts back to what mattered, forcing himself to focus on the cold, harsh, unexpected reality that had nothing to do with how much he'd enjoyed their leash-and-fall incident:

Damn, she'd actually turned him down!

He made himself stand still and not run after her, needing time to regroup and cool his blood. He couldn't deny that he admired the hell out of her at this moment. Okay, so her pigheadedness was pretty irritating, but he had to appreciate the pride he'd seen burning like hot coals in her eyes. She had principles. He liked that.

But what he liked—and it was becoming clear he really liked a lot of things about Sunny Williams—didn't matter. What mattered was that she was walking away.

He rubbed his chin, acknowledging that his priorities had changed in a big hurry. But he'd blown it and he had no idea how to fix things.

He'd always been more comfortable immersing himself in books than talking to people; even as a boy, he'd spent hours reading science books by himself, hoping to make a connection with his father by learning as much as he could about medicine. Personal relationships weren't his forte.

He started walking back to his office, looking at his problem from a practical viewpoint. The truth was, he needed Sunny Williams in a way that went far beyond his desire to have her laying on top of him again. Now, he just had to figure out a way to talk her into changing her mind—for the sake of becoming a medical researcher and jettisoning Mr. Commitment back to his dad, of course.

Chapter Three

Sunny gave up all pretense of calm and stomped back to her van, absolutely infuriated that her hopes to make a new start in Oak Valley had completely faded. Not to mention that she'd almost caved in to her impetuous side, given into temptation and welcomed Connor's kiss. Yes, her aura was probably glowing a fiery red right now.

It was impossible to ignore how irritating—yet knock-her-down attractive—Dr. Connor Forbes was proving to be. The man would test the patience and control of a saint.

As maddening as he was, there was something indescribable about him that she found really, really appealing. Darn the man! He was her total opposite and clearly had different values. But she simply couldn't deny that she found him incredibly attractive. His smile was enough to inspire goose bumps and a glance from his gorgeous green eyes set fires all over her. What *would* it be like to actually kiss him? Or lie in his arms, whispering her hopes and dreams to him, wrapped in a cocoon of warmth and security that would last forever?

What? She jerked her thoughts away from something so stupid as actually kissing exasperating, so-wrong-for-her Connor Forbes, much less finding the kind of commitment and stability she wanted with such a disagreeable man. Instead, she focused on her current situation.

She had no reason to stay in Oak Valley now. She was broke with no prospects. Maybe she'd have to ask her parents for help again.

She bit her lip, hating the idea of needing—let alone having to ask for—her parents' help. They'd always been hands-off, do-your-own thing parents, even when she'd longed for them to be more involved. From an early age they'd always encouraged her to go her own way and fulfill her own dreams. So she'd tried, but had failed all over the place, including her latest business debacle in San Francisco, which had involved barely escaping from bankruptcy after she'd overborrowed and underplanned when opening Sunny's Holistic Health Mart.

She'd never been able to find the kind of tremendous success her parents had. While she had been moving out of her rented store space in San Francisco, barely a dollar to her name, her parents had been accepting their fifth award as the California Marriage Counselors of the Year.

All she wanted to do was make them proud, to show them that she could take the independence they'd so willingly given her and make something of her life, something that mirrored their own accomplishments. Given that, going to them for help again just didn't seem right. Hopefully, she could make something happen on her own, find a job that would last longer than a year.

She reached the boardwalk, saddened by how much she already loved Oak Valley's wonderful, small-town atmosphere. She could easily picture her own office in a picturesque place like this. How wonderful it would have been to have people wandering in and out from the quaint boardwalk. To become a part of a place where everybody knew everybody. A place where she imagined committed, close-knit families held old-fashioned barbecues on the Fourth of July.

Muttering under her breath, "Darn the stubborn man anyway," she reached her van and heard a woman's voice call her name. She looked around and saw Jenny waving as she walked toward her, pushing a stroller that contained a towheaded toddler dressed from head to toe in pale yellow.

"Hey," Jenny said, smiling. "I'm glad I caught you."

Sunny stepped onto the boardwalk and clamped her gaze onto the little girl looking curiously up at her, her blue eyes wide and inquisitive. "And who is this big girl?" Sunny asked, squatting down to the adorable girl's level.

"This is Ava," Jenny replied. "Ava, can you wave to Sunny?"

Ava waved, grinning to expose two new teeth.

Sunny's heart melted and a lonely, empty place inside of her throbbed. Oh, how she wanted a family of her own, a passel of kids she could raise in a place like this with a steady, loving man by her side. That long-held dream was even more of a fantasy now.

"What's wrong?" Jenny asked. "You look so sad." She frowned, suddenly looking fierce. "My brother didn't do something to upset you, did he?"

Sunny rose and forced a smile, not wanting to burden Jenny with her problems. "No, of course not."

Jenny reached down and pulled a loose barrette from Ava's hair. "So did you manage to pound some sense into his thick skull?"

Sunny gave her a wry smile. "Is that possible?"

"Probably not, but I saw the way he looked at you…"

Good heavens, had she seen them in the park? "Whoa, ho, hold it," Sunny said. "What do you mean?"

Jenny gave an exaggerated shrug, then bent and replaced the barrette in Ava's hair. "Oh, just that I thought he might cut you some slack because he thinks you're hot."

A shaft of pleasure bolted through Sunny, but she ignored it, wanting to roll her eyes. Connor's so-called attraction sure hadn't worked in Sunny's favor in the career department. She gave Jenny a stern look. "Would you stop? Connor and I…uh, well, we worked out our problems, sort of."

"So you're staying?" Jenny asked, an enthusiastic glow in her eyes.

This situation was getting sticky. She didn't want

Jenny charging to her rescue any more than she wanted Connor's dad bailing her out. Connor needed to be the one to do the bailing, and he'd already proven he wasn't willing to for the good of his patients in the long term.

But she couldn't lie to Jenny. It would be obvious that Sunny had backed out of the deal when she left. She owed her an honest explanation. "No, I'm not. Actually, things…didn't go that well."

"Oh, no. So you're leaving?"

Sunny nodded and smiled, trying to look upbeat. "But don't worry. Something else will turn up."

Jenny placed a hand on her arm. "I wish you'd stay. Oak Valley would be the perfect place for you to live."

Sunny looked away for a moment, a lump forming in her throat. She couldn't help but notice how green the trees a block off Main Street looked, so fresh and vibrant against the crystal-clear blue sky, and how the bright flower baskets lining the boardwalk waved in the soft breeze.

From the moment she'd driven into town, she'd sensed that this place was just the spot to make her dreams come true. But perfect place or not, she was broke. She couldn't afford to stay unless she had a job. She was going to have to level with Jenny.

"Look, I can't stay. To be honest, I'm broke, I have nowhere to live and I need a job. I've got to go where those things can happen."

Surprisingly, a huge smile formed on Jenny's face. "But you *can* stay," she said, an eager light coming to life in her eyes. "With my parents. They have plenty of room, and I know they'd love to have you."

Sunny stared at Jenny, deeply touched by her offer, wishing she could take her up on it. But living with the Forbeses wouldn't solve her problems any more than agreeing to some short-term deal with Connor would. She needed a long-term job, not temporary living quarters, and she wouldn't feel right about barging in on the Forbeses who, while surely kind, she'd never even met. All of her communication with the elder Dr. Forbes had been by e-mail or through her parents. "That's very nice of you, but no. I couldn't impose, really."

Jenny waved her hand in the air. "Trust me, it's not an imposition. My folks have a carriage house that's been converted to a garage. It has an upstairs apartment we've all used at one time or another. In fact, last month, my brother, Aiden, and his new wife, Colleen, stayed there for a few days while they looked at property here in Oak Valley."

"You have another brother living in town?"

"No, not yet. They didn't find anything they were interested in, so they decided to stay in Aiden's house in Portland for the time being. But my guess is as soon as Colleen's pregnant, they'll be looking again."

Sunny's heart throbbed at the mention of another happy couple. Ignoring the ache in her chest, she said, "While I appreciate your offer, I have to say no."

Jenny gave her a stern glare, but her hazel eyes twinkled. "Oh, come on. Why don't you come with me, have lunch with my folks and then make a decision?"

Biting her lip, Sunny thought about Jenny's offer. What was the harm in having lunch with the Forbeses? A few hours' delay wasn't going to hurt her job search, and Jenny's dad had been very kind to her. She owed him an explanation, in person, about why she wasn't taking the job.

She looked at Jenny and lightly touched Ava's chubby little hand. "All right. You've talked me into it." She gestured to her van. "Should I drive?"

"That's fine, go on ahead. I don't have a car seat for Ava and this is my daily attempt to stay fit, so I'll meet you there." She gave directions to her parents' home, seven blocks away, and then looked down the board-walk, narrowing her eyes. "Uh-oh, Connor alert," she said, nodding behind Sunny.

Sunny turned around. Sure enough, Connor was walking toward her on the boardwalk two blocks down. Sunny's face heated and her tummy clenched when she thought about facing him after their close-kiss encounter. "Oh, great. I thought I was through with him."

Jenny put a hand on Sunny's arm and said, "You are. So don't tell Mr. Party Pooper about coming to my parents' house. Leave him in his own little clueless world, all right?"

Sunny nodded, biting her lip. "Okay."

"I'll see you at my parents' soon," Jenny said, push-ing the stroller around Sunny. "Wave bye-bye, Ava." Ava lifted a chubby hand and Sunny waved back, the knot of apprehension in her stomach growing. Boy, she hated feeling so nervous and off balance all the time, but it seemed the good doctor had that effect on her.

Determined to act normal, she opened the van's hatch and pointed inside. "Get in, Rufus."

Rufus yanked back on the leash and dug his paws into the road, refusing to obey.

Sunny rolled her eyes. "Oh, come on, you big oaf." She pulled the leash, but he pulled back harder. She knew this drill. Sighing, she lifted Rufus up, trying to push him into the van.

"Get…into…the…car…you…big…lug." He knew the drill, too, though, and went one-hundred-pounds-of-dog limp, his paws hanging over her arm, his front end on the tailgate of her van and his back end sagging to the ground.

Connor sauntered up and stood, watching, his hands pushed casually into his pockets.

Huffing and puffing, she glared at him. "I could use some help, here."

"Okay." He stepped closer. "You take the front, I'll take the back."

Rufus fought them, doing everything in his power to avoid getting in. But Connor's brute strength won out. *Very impressive,* Sunny thought, intensely aware of his large, muscular body working so closely to hers. Together, grunting with effort, they managed to stuff Rufus into the van, his paws skidding along the floor.

"Quick, slam the hatch!" Sunny instructed.

Connor obliged and closed the van before Rufus could make an escape.

Breathing heavily, Sunny sagged back against the van's door. "Thanks. Once he's out, he doesn't like to get back in."

Connor put a hand on the van next to her and leaned on it, making her very, very aware of how big and male he was. "I can see that. He needs major obedience training." His gaze held on her, his intense green eyes moving over her face. "Listen, I'd like to talk about this a little more."

She waved a negligent hand in the air. She had to ignore how his look and nearness sent hot tingles down her spine and another nameless feeling into her chest. Stupidly, he made her wish he'd just pull her close and tell her everything was going to be okay. "Nah, that's okay. He's in now—"

"Not the dog," Connor said, swiping a hand through his hair. "I meant I wanted to talk about you turning my offer down."

She was hoping to avoid another conversation by acting obtuse. No such luck. Pushing away, needing to get away from his rampant maleness and piercing gaze, she walked around the back of the van to the driver's door and said, "There's nothing to talk about. You don't respect what I do. I won't work under those conditions. End of story."

He followed her, his hands spread wide. "But you're cutting off your nose to spite your face," he said. "That's noble, maybe, but dumb, too."

She whirled on him, now more sure than ever that she'd made the right decision to walk away. "No, it's not dumb. And what's wrong with being noble?"

"Nothing, if you live in a fantasy world."

"Fantasy world?" she said, clenching her teeth. His sensible, stick-in-the-mud attitude drove her crazy. "What century were you born in? Are you always so disgustingly practical?"

He lifted one broad shoulder. "Yup."

She stomped her foot. "Yup!? Is that all you can say?" She swung away. "Listen to you," she said, gesturing wildly in the air with her hands. "All you can think about is being sensible and realistic." She turned back and looked at him. "Where's your heart?"

He gave her a blank look, then shook his head. "Just because I like to be sensible doesn't mean I don't have a heart. And while we're on the subject, are you always so ridiculously idealistic?"

She shoved her chin in the air. "Yes, I am, and proud of it. So, there you go—you've figured out the answer to your own question. You're radically practical, I'm intensely idealistic. It doesn't take a genius to see that a partnership would never work out, which is exactly what you're hoping for so you can boot me out in three months."

She opened the car door. "And just for the record, I may be noble and idealistic, but I'm not stupid. You might think it's dumb, but I can't work with someone who doesn't respect me, not even for three months." She climbed in and plopped down. "So take that and shove it through your sensible, oh-so-practical brain. Maybe, if you're lucky, you'll understand eventually." She yanked the door closed, hooked her seat belt and started the engine. "But I doubt it," she muttered under her breath.

Connor stepped onto the boardwalk, shaking his head. He waved, a quick, short jerk of his hand, then turned and walked toward his office.

Sunny looked at him, mad that he had such a nice, tight butt, such broad, strong-looking shoulders and that just one look from those eyes of his spread tingles all over her body.

Boy, did she wish he weren't so darned attractive, that he didn't draw her in so easily while pushing all of her buttons at the same time.

She dropped her head onto the steering wheel. "He drives me crazy," she mumbled. "Forget him."

A few seconds later, she raised her head, fighting the urge to stomp on the gas pedal and peel out. Instead, she took a deep, cleansing breath, let a car go by, then calmly pulled out into the street, deliberately pushing the difficult doctor from her mind.

As she drove, a question nagged at her. How smart was it to spend any time with the Forbeses, who would undoubtedly remind her how much she wanted to settle in a perfect town like Oak Valley? Connor had just graphically illustrated why she couldn't accept his deal. She had to move on. Her need for success demanded it.

She'd just have to be sure to be realistic about her current situation, no matter how charming and inviting the Forbes clan proved to be, no matter how much she wanted to put down roots here.

Unfortunately, Oak Valley wasn't the place to make

her dreams come true, much less fulfill her end of the pact by her thirtieth birthday.

Sunny drove her van up the long gravel driveway that led to the Forbes residence. When the house came into view, she couldn't help but smile. The blue Victorian two-story house, complete with a wide, white front porch, lovely, expansive yard, and a mammoth oak tree with a tire swing, was just the kind of old-fashioned, peaceful place she'd love to live in.

"Boy, Rufus, wouldn't it be wonderful to live here?"

Rufus woofed, then moved to the other side of the van, wagging his tail.

As she pulled closer, she noted the carriage house Jenny had mentioned on the far side of the house. There were wooden stairs leading up to the upper level, which looked to be plenty big enough for her and Rufus.

Wait a minute. What was she thinking? She'd only come here to apologize to the elder Dr. Forbes, not to fantasize about staying here.

Her gaze caught on a gray-haired man dressed in jeans and an Oregon Duck sweatshirt climbing out of a late-model SUV next to the garage. Undoubtedly Connor's father. He saw her pulling up and waved, his face wreathed in smiles.

Sunny stopped the van and cut the engine, then opened the door and stepped out, biting her bottom lip. Did this Dr. Forbes have any idea who she actually was or even that she was coming to lunch?

Dr. Forbes walked toward her. "You must be Sunny."

Sunny walked forward, smiling, relieved her appearance wasn't totally unexpected. "Yes, I am." She extended her hand and he shook it.

"I've heard so much about you from your parents." He gestured for Sunny to proceed to the porch, then looked down the road leading to the house. "Is Jenny coming back?"

"Yes, but she didn't have a car seat for Ava—your granddaughter is adorable, by the way—and she wanted to get some exercise by walking back." She sent Dr. Forbes an apologetic glance. "She sort of invited me for lunch. I hope you don't mind."

He waved a hand in the air and walked toward the porch steps. "Not at all. It's the least I can do for Connor's new partner."

Sunny followed, her stomach twisting. Obviously, Dr. Forbes was under the impression that the partnership between Sunny and Connor was working out, putting Sunny in an awkward position. Did she keep quiet and let Connor break the news, or speak up now, letting Dr. Forbes in on the current situation?

Sunny hated keeping secrets, and certainly didn't want him to think she'd deliberately kept him in the dark about her and Connor. "Actually, it doesn't look like Connor and I will be partners after all, Dr. Forbes. Things…uh, well, things didn't work out."

He opened the front door and looked back, frowning. "Why don't we have a seat in the living room and discuss this." He moved through the foyer into the tasteful living room, decorated in navy blue, maroon and cream.

"What happened? He was supposed to find you and eat crow."

She followed him into the living room. Now she knew where Jenny had come by her straight-talking ways. "Well, he found me, and he did eat crow, sort of. But the deal didn't work out." She hated to be truthful but it was necessary. "To put it bluntly, he has no respect for my work, Dr. Forbes. A three-month trial period would be a waste of time. He'd have me out on my ear the second those ninety days were up."

Dr. Forbes snorted and sat down on the floral print couch. "Darn him anyway. He could at least *try* to make this work."

"Oh, he did, in his own sort of backward way." She sat on an overstuffed blue chair next to the couch, her shoulders tightening. "This was my decision, not Connor's."

He leaned back and sighed. "I know how…arrogant my son can seem at times. I can understand why you wouldn't want to agree to this deal."

He gazed at her for a long moment, then leaned forward and rested his elbows on his knees. "Would you please reconsider? Connor's being stubborn, but underneath the bluster is a brilliant man who will eventually see the value of what you do."

She desperately wanted to believe him. Staying in Oak Valley would solve all of her problems, not to mention being the realization of at least part of her dream. "How can you be so sure?"

He rose and went over to look out the window. "Because I know my son." He turned back. "He'll come around eventually. Please reconsider."

She sat back, thinking about what the senior Dr. Forbes had said. She still hadn't fulfilled her end of the pact to be married by the time she was thirty. She didn't want to start over somewhere else. Oak Valley was where she instinctively believed she would find the life she was looking for.

And she trusted that Dr. Forbes Sr. knew Connor well enough to be able to predict what he would do. Plus, proving the value of what she did to Mr. Scientific would be a challenge she would welcome. He needed a wake-up call, and she relished being the one to show him how wrong he was.

True, she would have to deal with her ridiculous physical attraction to Connor. But she could handle that if she simply remembered that even though his masculine appeal pulled her in, he was one hundred and eighty degrees from the man she wanted.

"All right," she said, nodding, her shoulders relaxing. Thank goodness she wouldn't have to move on. Yet. "You've convinced me. I'll stay."

He smiled. "Good. I have a feeling you're just what my son needs."

Sunny raised a brow. "For his business, you mean, right?"

"Uh, right, right," he replied, a shade too guiltily, waving his hands in the air. "Business, that's it."

Sunny stood, peering at him. Was Mr. Forbes up to a little matchmaking? She wanted to be sure nobody in this family held out hope for a romantic relationship between her and Connor. She might be physically attracted to him, but that's as far as she would let it go. "Dr. Forbes, I may be way off base here, but I want you to know up front that Connor and I will never be more than business partners."

At his puzzled, almost disbelieving look, she held up a hand and continued. "I do want to settle down and commit to a man, but Connor isn't that man. He's much too repressed and judgmental, and it's obvious we don't have the same values."

He nodded. "I can see why you say that, but you haven't known him very long. Underneath his prickly exterior is a wonderful, caring man. He just doesn't know how to show it very well."

For a split second, the thought of uncovering that wonderful man intrigued and excited her. And the heady appeal of a few sizzling kisses along the way, followed by the murmured words of love and commitment she craved so badly, was undeniable.

Forget it. Dr. Disagreeable wasn't the kind of down home, in-touch-with-his-feelings kind of guy she was looking for. "I hate to disappoint you but…I don't want you getting your hopes up for something that will never be, all right?"

Disappointment flashed in his eyes, but he nodded and said, "All right."

Sunny moved toward the entryway. "Well, I guess if I'm staying, I'll need a place to live. I'd better get on that." She wouldn't feel right about mentioning Jenny's offer to stay above the carriage house. Dr. Forbes had already done enough to help her.

He stood and followed her into the foyer. "You know, Sheila and I decided you should stay here. We have a small apartment above the garage that would be the perfect place for you."

Sunny blinked. "Oh, I don't know. I wouldn't want to impose, and my dog—he's a Great Dane—might be a problem."

"It's not an imposition. It's the least we can do considering how much trouble Connor's put you through. And don't worry about the dog. We're all dog lovers here. He'll fit in just fine."

She bit her lip. In reality, staying here would be the perfect solution, and she couldn't ignore that he was the second person in the Forbes family to offer her the apartment. She was a firm believer in kismet. Perhaps staying here with the Forbes was meant to be. "All right, but I insist on paying rent." When he opened his mouth to speak, undoubtedly to refuse, she shook her head and said, "I insist. You're already paying for the lease on my office space. This is the least I can do."

He stared at her for a moment, looking a little put out. Then he grinned. "You drive a hard bargain." He walked over and held out his hand. "Deal. Plan on sharing all of your meals with us, too. As long as you're paying rent you might as well enjoy Sheila's delicious home cooking."

She shook his hand and returned his genuine smile, the joy of victory spreading through her. She would be able to stay in this wonderful little town, and perhaps find the perfect man to share her life with. Just as Robbie had found the perfect woman for him, even though that perfect woman wasn't her.

Even though she'd have to work with Connor, that would be it—work only. At the end of the day, she could leave him and his sexy green eyes, appealing smile and grumpy, antiquated attitudes behind. She would be able to return to this wonderful home and enjoy quiet evenings here, soaking up the kind of family atmosphere she craved, surrounded by people who were committed to each other.

Yes, considering how badly things had started out today, everything had worked out all right.

"I'm so glad that's settled," Dr. Forbes said, rubbing his hands together. "Wait till Connor comes home and hears the news. He'll be really surprised."

She pulled in her chin. "What do you mean, when Connor comes home?"

"Oh, didn't you know?" he said with an unmistakable gleam in his eyes. "Connor's remodeling a home he bought a few blocks away. Until it's done, he's staying here in his old room." He smiled broadly. "We'll all be one big, happy family."

She stared at him, understanding dawning. Why, the crafty, matchmaking man! Within seconds the lump of worry that had begun to form in her stomach exploded into a full-fledged boulder of sheer dread.

As she vaguely wondered why Connor was living in his old room rather than above the carriage house, the reality of her new living situation crashed down around her. Not only would she be working with Connor, the most attractive yet infuriating man she'd met in ages, she'd be living close to him, too. Same breakfast table. Same office. Same *everything*.

Her gut twisted. Dr. Forbes Sr. had maneuvered her into a corner. She was broke. She needed this job. She had to succeed to make her parents proud. A pact was a pact.

She had no choice but to live here with handsome, irritating Connor a constant distraction and huge temptation almost impossible for her to ignore.

Oh, boy. What kind of trouble had she gotten herself into now?

Chapter Four

Returning from an afternoon run, Connor ran up the driveway that led to his parents' house, the coarse gravel uneven beneath his pounding feet. At least he didn't have to deal with one alluring Sunny Williams at his office tomorrow. Or ever. Even though he hadn't exactly loved putting a kink in her plans, it was best this way. No partner. No attraction. Practical. Just the way he wanted things.

When he rounded the bend, the house came into view. An unfamiliar red van sat at the end of the driveway.

He frowned. Was that Sunny's van? Had Jenny intervened after all?

He took the porch stairs two at a time, clenching his jaw, wishing Jenny had minded her own damn business for once.

He slowed to a walk and opened the front door, noting the smell of garlic chicken, his mom's specialty, in the air. He moved up the hall and stepped into the kitchen.

Sure enough, Sunny was sitting at the kitchen table with his dad, a glass of his mother's homemade lemonade sitting in front of her, a glorious smile lighting her lovely face. His dad had his own glass in his hand, and his mom was standing at the stove, stirring something.

All three turned and looked at him. Sunny's smile faded and she simply sat there, staring at him for a long, wide-eyed moment. Then her gaze flicked down over his body before darting back up to hold on his nose. An appealing blush spread across her face and it looked like she liked what she saw. A lot. An answering warmth pooled in his belly. Too bad it couldn't be so simple as him and her in a hotel room for a weekend.

His dad raised his glass in greeting. "Hey, Connor. Look who's here." He smiled smugly and gestured to Sunny with his other hand. Great. His dad was yanking his chain.

Sunny waved, a single, short cut of her hand in the air, and gave Connor an awkward-looking smile. His mom glanced between him and Sunny, grinned, and kept stirring.

Connor moved into the kitchen, angry at being manipulated by his dad, and said the first thing that came to mind. "What's going on?"

"Well, hello to you too," his dad retorted. "Jeez, Con, have some manners."

Connor pressed his mouth into a tight line. "Well, I usually do when I'm not being ambushed."

His dad rose. "Ambushed? What do you mean?"

"Just that you seem to have some grand plan in mind, and you're determined that I be part of it."

"The only plan I have is to improve the standard of medical care in Oak Valley," his dad said. "Sunny could help with that, but you tried to run her out of town."

"I did not." Connor shook his head and avoided looking at Sunny, who suddenly seemed very interested in her lemonade. "I laid out the offer and she wasn't interested."

His dad shot a razor-sharp glare his way. "And I'm sure you used your usual amount of tact when you did it, right?"

Connor held up his hands in surrender. "Okay, I admit I may not have made the offer particularly gracefully." He clamped his back teeth together and looked away for a second, wishing this whole problem would just go away. "But it was her decision to turn it down."

His dad drained his lemonade and set the glass on the counter with a thump. "Don't get yourself in a knot. Doesn't matter anyway." He glanced back at Sunny and grinned. "Sunny's changed her mind."

Connor dropped his jaw slightly, stared at his dad for a few moments and then skipped his gaze to Sunny. She smiled and nodded quickly, confirming his dad's announcement. To her credit, she didn't look smug or as if she was gloating. In fact, she looked pretty uncomfortable.

Connor switched gears. Things had changed. Sunny *was* going to be his partner.

No problem, right? He had to remember that there was an upside to this whole deal. His dad might return from retirement, allowing Connor time to pursue a job in medical research. He might be able to hand Mr. Commitment back over to his dad eventually. All in all, this news wasn't so bad.

Except gorgeous, engaging Sunny would be by Connor's side at work. All day. Every day. Heat suffused his already warm body and he held back a groan. His new partner would be a constant temptation he would have to work damn hard to ignore.

Connor only hoped he would be able to make it through the day, come home and forget about how much he wanted to see if her hair was as soft as it looked, how she smelled up close and what it would be like to kiss those pink lips. Over and over again.

His dad spoke again, interrupting Connor's stupid thoughts. "Best of all, Sunny's found a place to live."

Connor looked at his dad, his eyes narrowed, a bad feeling creeping up on him. "Really," he said as casually as he could. "Where?"

His dad slapped him on the back. "Why, right here, son. She's going to be living over the garage."

Connor's stomach fell. Suddenly the deal, no matter how much it would help him in the long run, was nowhere near a good idea after all.

Sunny staying here was going to cost him.

Connor looked like he was about to throw up.

Sunny could identify. She hadn't been very happy to

discover she would be living with him, either. But given the state of her finances, if she was going to stay in Oak Valley, living here was her only option, even though being under the same roof, or nearly so, with a hot guy like Connor was going to be a challenge.

Unable to help herself, Sunny glanced at him from under her lashes as he talked to his mom, her blood heating, her nerves revving up. How had she ever thought of him as *scholarly?* Standing across the kitchen dressed in running shorts and a faded blue T-shirt with the arms cut out he looked more like a hunky stud than the studious bookworm she'd pegged him as. His long, lightly tanned, muscular legs, sculpted arms and broad, firm-looking shoulders screamed fit, healthy, vibrant guy.

And nothing appealed to her more than a man who took care of himself.

She forced her interested gaze away, fighting the urge to fan herself with her hand and squirm. So he was in shape. Big deal. She wasn't interested in him at all. She could deal with his blatant maleness.

Couldn't she?

She bit her lip and drummed her fingers on the oak table. Fate had dealt her this hand, and she had no alternative but to play the cards, even though he made her insides sweat.

She sighed, then looked at Connor again, careful to focus on his face rather than his perfectly put-together, totally hot body.

He stared back, his eyes homing in on hers like an emerald laser. A hot chill skated up her spine, and even though she wanted to look away, she couldn't. His eyes flicked down and held on her breasts for a bare second; then he looked back up, snagging her gaze again.

Heaven help her, the doctor was a red-blooded man beneath the aloof, tightly wound exterior. Her nipples tightened and her lower body throbbed. Through the haze of sexual sensations flooding her body, one thought rang clear. Jenny was right! Connor was looking at her like a very, very interested male.

An answering pulse of attraction roared through her, heating her whole body. Resisting the urge to fan herself, she shifted on the chair. Finally, she ripped her gaze away and looked down at her lap briefly, praying her face wasn't as red as it felt.

Connor mumbled something under his breath, made an abrupt about-face and then excused himself to take a shower. Sunny breathed a sigh of temporary relief, very deliberately forcing her mind away from the thought of a soapy, naked Connor showering on the next floor up. She poured imaginary ice water on the fire in her blood and plastered a fake smile on her face, prepared to be like her mother, who was a master at the serene routine when life got complicated. Sunny would go with the flow and pretend that everything was just fine.

Even though that was as far from the truth as it could be.

Connor showered and dressed, telling himself that the sizzling look that had passed between him and Sunny in the kitchen didn't mean anything except that he was a normal man reacting to a beautiful woman. Nothing wrong with that. In fact, he would be more worried if he *didn't* have a sexual reaction to her.

Feeling better about his physical attraction to Sunny, he methodically went over the situation in his head. He was going to have to find a way to deal with living in close quarters with Sunny for the next three months without going crazy.

Be rational. Yes. Once he looked at his problem in a rational way, the answer was a no-brainer. He would just have to find a way to spend as little time here as possible. Luckily, between his work and the remodeling of the house he'd bought, he would have plenty of other things to think about besides a pair of stunning brown eyes and hair like liquid gold.

Satisfied he had everything under control, including his raging hormones, he joined his parents and Sunny for dinner, doggedly trying not to get sucked into admiring Sunny's bright, engaging smile and the cute jokes she told at the table and how she made his parents laugh. Why couldn't she be a dull conversationalist with a gap-toothed smile?

Following his plan, and needing space, he quickly ate, excused himself with a word to his mom to leave the dishes, his usual job, and left to return to his office to catch up on some paperwork.

He walked downtown and immersed himself in files for an hour and a half, then spent an hour rearranging the already neat bookshelf in his office and organizing his medical journals by name, year and month. He then went over his patient files for the next day and reread an article on a new drug for asthma.

Finally, at nine-thirty, he ran out of inane tasks. At this rate, he was going to have the most organized office on the planet. He looked around and smiled. Could be worse.

He walked home, his breath misting the air around him, letting his mind wander to any subject but Sunny Williams. She was a temptation he couldn't give in to, a test he refused to fail. Despite his raging need for a little casual female companionship, he had to keep his distance.

He headed up the driveway. Man, he hoped she was already in her room above the garage. The last thing he wanted to deal with was her sexy, appealing presence.

No such luck. When the house came into view, he saw her sitting on the porch swing alone, gazing up at the clear autumn night sky.

Right on cue, his blood began to heat. Shaking his head, he tamped down his body's response and kept walking. He would just casually say hello and saunter right on by.

He mounted the porch steps and looked her way, noticing right off how her hair shimmered from the darkened porch in the light of the full moon.

She waved. "Hey, Connor," she said, her husky voice humming across the air, setting his nerves on edge. She pushed her hair back with one hand. He could imagine her breasts lifting underneath her shirt…

He stopped, clenching his back teeth together. "Sunny." He noticed the blanket she had wrapped around her shoulders. "It's cold." He moved a bit closer, wondering how close he would have to get before her alluring scent hit him. "What are you doing out here?"

She pointed to the moon. "Looking at that. It's beautiful, don't you think?"

He looked up, but couldn't see the moon from where he was standing. He bent down and took a quick look, then raised one shoulder and let it fall. "Yeah, I guess so."

"Oh, come on." She stood, leaving the blanket, and beckoned him closer. "Look from over here," she said, moving toward the porch railing.

He hung back, not sure he should let himself get any closer. He was going for uninterested and uninvolved here. Any closer and his body would definitely be involved. "It's just the moon," he said, moving a little nearer. "No big deal."

She looked at him, a tiny frown on her face. "I know, but it's particularly bright and close tonight." She took two large steps and gripped his hand before he knew what she was doing. Tugging gently, she said, "Boy, do you need to loosen up."

Her small, warm hand sent sparks radiating up his arm into his chest. He reluctantly followed, unable to resist her pull.

When they reached the railing, she pointed up again, smiling. "There. Now look at that and tell me it's not beautiful."

Very aware of her hand still in his, mainlining heat into his body like a drug, he did as she asked and looked up. The gold-tinged moon hung bright and low in the clear, dark night sky, surrounded by thousands of stars.

He stared, trying to see it from her perspective. He didn't usually take the time to look at stuff like this, but even to him, the moon did look good tonight.

Turning, he glanced down at her, noting again how pretty her hair looked, how lovely her profile was. Even though he knew that he shouldn't let himself get caught up in her, she was so damn appealing he couldn't seem to help himself. His hands itched and he had the sudden urge to run his hand along the delicate curve of her jaw. "Beautiful," he murmured before he could stop his thoughts from turning into words.

She met his gaze. "I…I was talking about the moon," she whispered.

Her tawny gaze slammed into him and he felt his control cut out. His blood pounding, wanting just one harmless touch, he brought his hand up to lightly stroke her jaw. Her skin was as soft as silk. "And I was talking about you," he said, hazily aware that he was sailing into treacherous waters but was seemingly unable to stop the ship and get off.

She blinked and then licked her plump, pink lips. Damn, he wanted to feel those lips against his own with every male cell in his body. With her standing there, gazing up at him, her lips glistening in the moonlight, holding back was as futile as trying to revive a dead man. She swayed nearer and he could have sworn he smelled her scent hovering in the air.

That downright sexy smell might as well have been

a baseball bat flying through the air, knocking all of his good judgment out of him. Giving in, he lowered his head and kissed her.

She turned when his lips touched hers and pushed her body up against his, snaking her arms around his waist with soft little sounds of delight. Fire exploded in his blood at the feel of her feminine curves pressed against him.

He gathered her closer, cupping the back of her head with one hand, gripping her curvy bottom with the other. Wanting more, he deepened the kiss, plying her lips open with his tongue, needing to taste her. She complied, stroking his tongue with her own.

"Connor?" his dad called from the front door.

Connor yanked away, breathing hard. Sunny stumbled back against the porch rail and raised a shaky hand to her lips, her eyes wide and stunned.

"Uh, yeah, Dad," he managed to say.

"Just wanted to be sure you were home."

"I'm home." He drew in a large breath of air. "Sunny and I were just…talking."

A long silence. "Oh. All right." His dad sounded like he was smiling. "Good night."

"Good night," Connor said, pacing away, trying to corral his untrustworthy control. Obviously, his healthy masculine side had homed in on an attractive female and taken over.

"Was it that bad?" Sunny asked.

He stopped and swung a curious gaze toward her. "What?"

"The…um, kiss."

"No, why would you ask that?" Actually, the kiss had been very, very good. Too good. Now he was sure all he'd be able to think about would be kissing her again.

She sat down on the porch swing and lifted one brow. "Because you look like you just tasted castor oil."

He swiped a hand through his hair. "No, no. The kiss was fine."

"Then tell me what you're so upset about."

He let out a heavy breath. So much for just saying hello and sauntering by. Now not only had he kissed her, but he had to talk to her about it, too.

Talking made sense, but he hated admitting to making a mistake. He moved over and leaned back against the porch railing. "Sunny…I guess what I need to say is that kissing you was a mistake."

She smiled but it didn't reach her eyes. "Gee, thanks. You really know how to crush a girl's ego."

"No. Not a mistake because it was bad. A mistake because…because I don't want any kind of romantic relationship."

He saw the raw confusion in her eyes. Damn, he owed her a cursory explanation for why he'd kissed her and pulled away. "I'd love to see where our kiss would lead." He gave her rueful smile. "But I can't let it go that far. I'm…attracted to you, and I've learned that that leads to failure. I have to stop this before I'm in too deep." He'd let himself go too deep too many other times with bad results—Julie in college, Sarah in med school, Allison in Seattle just a year ago—to let it happen again.

She nodded, looked at the porch floor and then pushed her hair in back of her ear with one hand. She looked up at him, a considering expression materializing on her face. "Do you mind if I ask why…you think you'll fail?"

Hell yes, he minded. He had no intention of talking about how every woman he'd ever gone out with had dumped him, how bad he was at romance. No guy wanted to admit to that. "Let's just say I that I hate failing, and never intend to again. Committing isn't for me."

Surprisingly, she gave him a wry smile. "Hmm. A Mr. Commitment who can't commit. Now there's an interesting concept."

He frowned. "I never wanted the title of Mr. Commitment." He lifted one shoulder and let it fall. "I guess you're right, though."

She moved away slightly and crossed her arms over her chest. "You were right to pull away." She turned and pierced him with her dark eyes. "You've just confirmed that you're the wrong man for me."

Her words cut through him like a rusty scalpel. "Why?" he asked before he could stop himself.

She uncrossed her arms. "Well, first, I do want to commit, more than anything in the world. Second, you're just not the kind of guy I want."

He bristled and opened his mouth to speak, but she held up a hand. "Hey, I know that sounds harsh, and I'm sorry. But please don't be offended. The truth is, you're too different from me. We obviously have different beliefs about medicine and you don't really respect what

I do. I can deal with that professionally, but not on a truly personal level."

He digested her words, trying not to let that scalpel cut too deep, surprised that it cut him at all. This was no big deal. She was being practical, doing what was best for her, and he admired that.

He let out a frustrated breath. He didn't want to like or admire her at all; it made keeping his necessary distance even more of a struggle.

Problem acknowledged. All that he needed to do was be levelheaded, focus on what was practical and he'd be fine.

He nodded. "Okay, so we're in agreement. While we're obviously attracted to each other, no more kissing, right?"

"Right," she said, nodding, looking pretty darned sure of her answer.

They stood in silence for a moment, the only sound the rustle of the light breeze through the paper birch trees next to the house. Connor fought the strange disappointment working its way through him, shoving it into its hole. He had to protect himself from failing again.

Then, with a small wave, she moved toward the porch steps. "I'm tired, so I think I'll go to bed now. Good night, Connor." She turned and walked down the steps, moving toward the carriage house and leaving him on the porch alone, with the cool autumn night as his only companion.

He looked out into the dark, trying not to dwell on the image of Sunny getting herself ready for bed—did she wear flannel, lace or nothing?—sternly reminding himself he should be glad they'd had this little discussion. He'd discovered where she stood, what she was looking for.

And it wasn't him.

Oddly, that thought stung and, damn it, created a hollow space inside of him he hated. He knew from experience that pursuing any kind of relationship with Sunny would end in failure and cold heartache. He didn't need any reminders about how love was the only thing he didn't do well.

He needed to remember that reality when he wanted to pull her close and bury his nose in her sweet-smelling hair before he worked his way to her mouth and kissed her again.

Pushing away that arousing thought, struggling to keep everything under control—just the way he liked it—he turned and went into the house, careful to close the door behind him, shutting out the temptation of Sunny. He climbed the stairs and ruthlessly shoved away the niggling thought that now that he'd kissed Sunny, forgetting how she felt in his arms was going to be damn near impossible.

Chapter Five

Three days later, Sunny walked to work early in the morning, elated she already had her first patient booked and satisfied she had her office set up reasonably well. Though the space was smaller than the office she'd had in San Francisco, she loved its warm coziness and knew her patients would feel at home there. She'd brought a lot of welcoming accessories with her, including sage-colored curtains that, luckily, fit the windows, matching area rugs to soften the linoleum floor and framed abstract pictures in taupe and cream. She'd even splurged on a can of closeout paint and painted the wall a warm, inviting shade called café au lait.

The storefront was small, so she intended on eventually moving her yoga classes to a larger space when she had a full class registered and could afford it. For now, she intended to focus on massage therapy in conjunction with the Forbes medical practice.

Even though she'd spent the last three days vowing not to think about Connor, inevitably her thoughts wandered to the sizzling kiss they'd shared on the porch in the moonlight. Try as she might, she simply couldn't forget how his mouth had felt on hers, how he'd smelled like a combination of man and spice, how good it had felt to be enfolded in his strong, muscular arms. His kiss had set her blood on fire and had made her want to drag him up to her room and tangle herself in the sheets with him. No man had ever affected her as profoundly as Connor had. Which was unfortunate.

She shook her head. She was a fool to dwell on Connor. She'd known from the moment she'd met him that he wasn't the kind of man she wanted, and he'd confirmed that when he'd told her that he never wanted to commit. End of story.

Determined to focus on the cool October morning rather than on Connor, she rounded the corner, wishing she'd made an earlier start instead of enjoying a second cup of coffee with Mrs. Forbes, or Sheila as she'd pestered Sunny to call her. While Sunny had been sitting in the kitchen with Sheila after she'd taken Rufus for a quick walk, Connor had come downstairs, looking better than any man had the right to look first thing in the morning, all freshly showered, his auburn-highlighted hair still slightly wet and his face newly shaved.

Stupidly, her heart had done a two-step in her chest when she'd seen him, a frustratingly common occurrence, and she'd fought the urge to drool. The wrong man for her or not, he always affected her physically, making her wish she could corner him on the porch again and kiss him until she couldn't breathe.

Her blood percolating, she'd stayed with Sheila until long after Connor had left, not wanting to follow his path to work, needing to keep her distance. Especially after Sunny had commented on the beautiful, hand-drawn charcoal pictures of local flowers Sheila had hanging in the kitchen. Imagine Sunny's surprise when Sheila had told her *Connor* had drawn them.

Talk about shaking up Sunny's world. Who would have imagined that stuffy, uptight Connor would have that kind of artistic talent? Was there more to the man underneath his reserved, grumpy exterior?

Ignoring that idea, Sunny had said goodbye to Sheila and headed to work, concentrating on her coming day rather than her unexpected discovery of Connor's artistic side. It felt so good to be back at work, helping people. She prayed this business would be a success when all of her other career endeavors had failed, that she'd made the smart, correct choice for once. She wanted so badly for her parents to be proud of her.

When she stepped onto the boardwalk she looked ahead. It looked like there were several people waiting in front of her office door.

Smiling, Sunny was pleased word of her practice was getting around—had the elder Dr. Forbes had a hand in that? She picked up the pace, eager to get to work. Just what she needed to forget Connor Forbes.

She waved and greeted the people in the small line and unlocked the door.

Her new life had officially begun.

Since he'd arrived at his office, Connor had done everything possible not to think about how beautiful Sunny had looked sitting in his mother's kitchen, dressed in a cream-colored sweater that showed off her curves and a flowing, floral print skirt.

The moment he'd seen her this morning, the erotic images that had been bothering him all night had come hurtling back into his brain and he'd been stuck on that arousing memory ever since. Man, she'd smelled good last night, sort of like a field of warm flowers, and she'd been so soft and eager in his arms. And her lips, well, her lips were unforgettable, so lush and welcoming.

He snapped a file closed and snorted, yanking his thoughts away from Sunny for the hundredth time, only to see the line of people that had formed—make that line of *men*—outside the window of his office.

Apparently word of Sunny's "services" had made its way through town, along with, he was sure, how beautiful the new massage therapist was.

An odd, kind of fiery feeling exploded inside of him. He frowned. What was his problem? Everything was going according to his keep-away-from-Sunny plan. He'd successfully avoided her for the last week.

So why was he so bugged? Why was he feeling so…territorial? Damn if he didn't have a wild impulse to go next door and see exactly what was going on.

He didn't have another patient for an hour, so he gave in to his stupid urge to check things out next door. Rising, he made his way out of his office, rounded the reception counter and stalked out the door with a wave to June. As Sunny's partner, he had a right to drop in, right?

The men in the line outside greeted him. He cut the air with his hand in a stiff wave before he yanked open Sunny's office door, which had a hand-painted, flowery Welcome sign hanging from a nail in the center panel.

He stepped through the door, excusing himself around a few more men, and immediately detected a scent that reminded him of Sunny—light, floral, intoxicating. Memories of their kiss hit him again. He grunted under his breath. Just his luck that the place smelled so much like her.

Trying to ignore the arousing scent lingering in the air, he looked around. He lifted his eyebrows, impressed by the transformation of the space from shabby, bare room to inviting, peaceful sanctuary.

She'd placed a wooden desk about eight feet from the back wall, facing out, to serve as a reception area, and had set up a row of fabric-covered screens behind the desk to create a sort of back office. Looking more closely at the desk, he recognized it was an old desk he'd seen in his parents' garage recently. Apparently his dad had meant it when he said he wanted to help her out.

A bouquet of fresh flowers sat on the desk and he noticed several others placed strategically around the room on small, fabric-draped tables.

Several men greeted him from the right side of the

room and he acknowledged them, noticing that Sunny had put several neutral-colored couches in the front corner to serve as her waiting area.

He'd seen the space before and knew that there was a small room to the rear, accessed by the door on the back wall. He deduced that she was using that room as her "examining" room.

As if to confirm that thought, the door opened and Sunny stepped out, followed by Steve McCarthy. Flames ignited in Connor's chest. He gritted his jaw. Why wasn't McCarthy at his vet clinic? The guy was smiling broadly and Sunny was grinning back at him.

Sunny saw Connor and looked surprised for just a moment before she pulled in her chin, frowning. Realizing he was scowling, Connor immediately relaxed his face, trying to look like he was simply her business partner checking things out.

She shook her head slightly, then led Steve to the front desk. She opened her appointment book and made another appointment for Steve, who looked fit and hearty and probably didn't need her services in the least. Steve then left, acknowledging Connor as he walked to the door.

Connor looked to Sunny. She hesitated briefly, her eyes wide, and then smiled at him. "Dr. Forbes," she said, inclining her head to the side. "What can I do for you?"

One thing she could do for him popped into his mind but he ignored it, barely. Instead, he scrambled for a believable answer. "I was just checking up on how things were going over here," he said in as professional a tone as he could manage.

She smiled serenely. "As you can see," she said, gesturing to the patients waiting, "everything is going just fine." She walked nearer, a glimmer of pleasure shining in her eyes. "I had no idea my massage therapy services would be in such high demand here in Oak Valley."

Connor fought the urge to snort. She obviously didn't have a clue that more than likely most of the men were here simply to check out the hot new masseuse in town.

He opened his mouth to tell her as much, but the words died when he saw how happy the fact that she had plenty of clients made her. Instead, he improvised and said, "Oh, yeah. You'll have lots of clients, I'm sure."

Her brilliant smile grew even brighter. Leaning close, she whispered, "You think so? I was worried about that."

He unwittingly took a breath that filled his head with her scent. His pulse pounding, he pointed to the crowd of patients waiting. "I don't think you have anything to worry about."

She looked relieved. "Oh, thank you for saying so." She placed her slender hand on his arm. "I was so worried about this. Things didn't go so well in San Francisco and my business went belly-up." She removed her hand. "Of course, this is only the second day of business, but I think I've made a good start, and that pleases me. I want so much to stay here in Oak Valley."

The spot she'd touched on his arm still warm, he let his gaze linger on her, his chest drawing tight. Yeah, he liked her bright smile and the satisfied, happy gleam in her gorgeous brown eyes.

"Looks like you're set," he said in answer to her

thanks, belatedly realizing that her possible success would make it difficult for him to cut her loose after three months. Funny how he'd automatically assumed she'd fail. Funny how the prospect of being the one to ruin her dream bugged him.

The door opened and Judd McDonald stepped in. Sunny excused herself and moved from Connor's side back to the reception desk and greeted Judd.

Connor stood there for a long moment, confused by his reaction to Sunny's happiness. He felt surprisingly bad about possibly ruining her dream of building a successful business in Oak Valley. He hadn't come here to be pleased because Sunny believed she was succeeding. He hadn't come here to enjoy her satisfied smile. He hadn't come here to raise niggling questions about his plan not to have a partner any longer than necessary.

But all of those things were true.

He couldn't ignore that Sunny's happiness lit up a space in his heart he wanted to keep dark.

And he couldn't overlook that he was a hell of a lot more interested in Sunny than he wanted to be.

That night, from the Forbeses' porch, with a smile and a wave goodbye, Sunny watched Steve McCarthy get in his truck, start the ignition and drive away.

It had been a good day.

Business was going well—she'd seen ten patients today and had had to rebook another five. Also, Steve, who could very well be her perfect, small-town man, had asked her to the town's annual Harvest Festival tomorrow night.

Was she one step closer to fulfilling the pact she'd made with Robbie?

She sat down on the porch swing, slightly ashamed to admit to herself that she'd harbored a secret, totally far-fetched fantasy that Connor would ask her to be his date for the dance.

She had to remember that *fantasy* was the key word in that thought. She would be smart to forget about dating Connor in any way, shape or form. She didn't really even like him. He definitely wasn't the right man for her, wasn't the guy to help her find the happiness Robbie had.

He wasn't the man to make her dreams come true.

Well, maybe a few dreams involving her bed, a naked Connor and—

"What was Steve doing here?" Connor asked from the porch steps, jerking her from her escalating erotic thoughts, starring him.

Her cheeks warm, Sunny looked at Connor, who was apparently returning from whatever it was he scurried off to do every night. Did he have a secret girlfriend stashed somewhere?

Setting that regrettably disturbing thought aside, she was embarrassed to admit she'd taken to sitting on the porch every night, foolishly hoping for a repeat of their sizzling kiss. Tonight was the first time since their last encounter on the porch that she'd caught him returning.

Taming the butterflies suddenly dive-bombing in her tummy, she tried for a smile. Hopefully, she looked as if Connor were the last thing on her mind. "He came to visit me."

Connor moved closer and then leaned back against the porch railing right next to the swing. "Business or pleasure?" he asked, his deep, smooth voice wrapping itself around her in a way she loved almost as much as she loved the feel of his strong arms around her. Boy, was she blowing this not-thinking-about-him thing, or what?

Very aware of how close Connor's large, muscular thigh was to her, she squirmed slightly on the swing, then hastily stood and moved a few large steps away from him, needing space to get a grip. "Pleasure." She smiled and looked him right in the eye, feeling safe from his male appeal at this distance. "He asked me to the Harvest Festival."

Connor stilled and his jaw fell the tiniest little bit. "He asked you out?"

She bristled. "Yes, he did. Why is that so hard for you to believe?"

He stared at her. "Believe me, it isn't." He yanked a hand through his disheveled hair and then paced away, his head bent, muttering something indecipherable under his breath.

Was he mad? Or…an astounding thought occurred to her. Maybe he was…jealous? She stared at him for a few seconds, tapping her chin, her eyes slightly narrowed. No way. She highly doubted the oh-so-practical Dr. Forbes, a man who was so against commitment and romantic relationships, would be jealous. Would he?

"You seem…bothered that Steve asked me out," she said, allowing herself to give in to a little harmless curiosity.

He gave her a remarkably dispassionate look. "It doesn't matter to me in the least that you're going to the Harvest thingy with Steve McCarthy."

An ache built in her chest. "That's what I thought." Suddenly, inexplicably deflated, she stepped back, reminding herself that she needed to keep a wall up between them all the time. She couldn't let herself get sucked into Connor's physical pull, or how his drawings had revealed a more in-touch, artistic side to his personality that intrigued her, or that it had become obvious over the last week that he was genuinely concerned about each and every one of his patients.

She switched gears to something less bothersome, remembering that she had a business matter to discuss with Connor.

She drew the blanket around her, feeling chilled. "Not to change the subject, but I've been meaning to talk to you about Edith Largo."

He swung his emerald gaze toward her, his brows drawn together. "She came to see you?"

Sunny nodded, trying not to let his skeptical reaction sting. "She's interested in my upcoming yoga classes."

He gave her a questioning look. "Okay. How does that involve me?"

"She's having problems with Danny," she said, "and I thought Mr. Commitment might be able to help."

Connor's face tightened. "I just saw her in my office with Danny last week and she didn't mention any problems."

"Well, I guess that's changed. I saw her yesterday,

and it didn't take her long to unload on me. She needs help, Connor, and admitted she wished your dad was still around the practice. She was near tears, frustrated over her inability to discipline Danny, who, she fears, is flunking fifth grade."

Connor shoved his hands in his pockets and looked at the floor. "I'm the wrong person to be dispensing relationship advice," he said, his mouth stiff, shaking his head. "My dad never should have turned Mr. Commitment over to me."

His admission of his inabilities and weaknesses touched her. "Would you like me to help you?"

He looked surprised, then stepped closer and searched her face. His eyes softened, sending a hot chill racing down her spine, totally disarming her. "You're still offering your help, even after I turned you down?"

"I guess I am," she said, very aware of the affect of his deep green gaze locked on her. Images of their hot kiss flashed through her brain, raising her temperature a notch. She pushed the blanket off her shoulders.

"Why?" he asked, yanking her attention back to their discussion.

Good question. Their relationship had been rocky from the start and he'd made no secret of how much he didn't respect her brand of healing. Why did she want to help him? Was it simply to ensure he still wanted her around after the obligatory three months? Or was it more than that?

She rose and paced away, stalling. She didn't want to read too much into her wanting to help him or admit that there might be more to her desire to help than simply business. Business was all that could matter between them.

Finally, she turned back to him, lifting a shoulder, attempting to look casual. "Why not? We're partners, right? Maybe I just want to prove myself. You've made no secret that you'd like to get rid of me as soon as you can."

"I was a jerk," he said, moving closer. "So you're saying you want to help me on a strictly business level, right? To prove yourself."

She nodded. "Right. And, of course, I want to help Edith and Danny."

He smiled, staring at her again, a knowing light in his eyes. "Right. Edith and Danny. As good a reason as any."

She stared back, warmth pooling in her lower body, feeling that there was an intimate subtext taking over their conversation. He continued to skim his gaze over her face. She clung to his intent stare, unable to summon up her self-control and look away. The dark, quiet night, broken only by the muted sound of a dog barking in the distance, fell down around her and the intimacy of the situation hit her full force. Memories of their kiss, on this very porch, slammed into her again and she had the urge to step close and turn her mouth up for another.

"Don't look at me that way," he warned, a dark, thrilling light rising in his eyes.

Her cheeks blazed. "What way?"

"Like you want to kiss me." He reached up to touch her cheek, but, disappointingly, he stopped and his hand fell away before he touched her. "Ah, damn. We both know this is wrong." He swung away, his eyes appearing full of regret, and shoved his hands in his coat pockets.

His words struck a chord in her. As much as she hated to turn away from him, he was right. She was playing with fire with the wrong kind of man. She had to keep her distance and back away.

She nodded, toying with the ends of her hair. "Good thing one of us has some sense, right?" she said, referring to him. "If you hadn't pointed out how wrong this situation was, I might have given in to my impulsive, wild side and kissed you senseless." Heat and a now familiar yearning she would have to learn to ignore filled her.

He stared at her for a long, breathtaking moment, raking his intense eyes over her from head to toe in a very unsensible, very male way, stoking a slow burning fire inside of her. For one impetuous beat in time, she hoped that he would ignore sense and kiss her. "Get any closer, look any more, Dr. Forbes, and sensible will fly right out the window."

He stilled and then held up his hands in mock surrender, smiling. "You've given me fair warning. I guess that's my cue to leave." He backed away, shaking his head. "I must be a fool to walk away from this. From you."

"No, you're no fool," she said, on the edge of calling him back and attacking him on the porch swing. "You're just smart, and I have to be smart for once, too."

He swiped a hand through his hair. "And smart means Steve McCarthy, not me."

As hard-hearted as that sounded, she had to nod. Connor had spoken the unvarnished truth, a truth she couldn't, in fairness to him, or herself, hide. "Yes…well, maybe. To the Steve part." She smiled apologetically. "Yes, definitely, to the you part," she whispered.

A shadow grew in his eyes and she hated that she'd put it there. But she was talking, ultimately, about her life here, her dream, fulfilling the pact and finding an anchor, and she had to take her choice seriously.

Feeling the need to explain, she said, "I want to commit and I need a man who wants the same thing. Realistically, there is no way to make you fit into that equation."

The shadow in his eyes darkened, but he nodded. "Okay, then, I'll go." He reached the door, paused, and said, "You're sure?"

She closed her eyes for a moment, gathered her sensibility and control together, willing away the need to give in to her crazy side and be close to him. She looked at him again and nodded, a brief, quick jerk of her head. "I'm sure."

He said nothing, just inclined his head in acknowledgment, opened the door and went inside, taking his warmth with him.

She was left sitting alone and cold on the porch swing, her body craving his touch, one tantalizing thought reverberating in her head: *What would he have done if I'd said I wasn't sure?*

She shoved that intriguing thought as far away as she could, intending to forget about Connor and focus instead on Steve, a man who was probably much more likely to be what Connor definitely wasn't.

A man to make her dreams come true.

Chapter Six

The dry weather changed, and the day of the Harvest Festival dawned with typical cool Oregon drizzle. Sunny spent the day at her office catching up on paperwork and small projects, thankful Connor had chosen to make a trip to Portland with his dad instead of working. She needed time away from him to drive home the idea that despite how physically attracted she was to him, she had to keep her distance.

The skies were cloudy and dull gray, and the light shining through the windows of her office was muted and pale. Sunny's mood matched the day—blah and ho-hum—and no matter how hard she tried, she couldn't seem to drag herself out of her melancholy doldrums.

When she headed home to change for the festival, she told herself she was going to make a concerted effort to enjoy herself with Steve. He was definitely a very attractive man in his own right, with his stocky build, blond hair and blue eyes, and seemed a much closer match to the stable, small-town man she was looking for than Connor was.

Steve came directly up to her little room above the garage to pick her up. He looked very handsome in what looked to be new Levi's, a cream-colored turtleneck and a brown leather coat, and he greeted a rambunctious Rufus like a long-lost friend.

As they walked to his truck, Sunny noted he had a wonderful smile and perfect manners and would undoubtedly prove to be a polite, considerate date. She doggedly ignored the fact that he didn't make her pulse explode like Connor did.

They drove to the festival, and arrived amid a bustling crowd. Steve explained that almost everybody in town turned out for the event.

They stepped into Oak Valley Community Center's gathering hall and it certainly looked as if the whole town was already there. The large room, decorated with hay bales, pumpkins, dried cornstalks and black, yellow and orange streamers, was filled to the brim with people of all ages and sizes.

A trio of fiddlers played upbeat music in one corner, and a long series of tables lined up along the far wall almost groaned with the weight of a potluck feast fit for a kingdom. The other side of the room held games and crafts for the kids, including a pumpkin-carving station set up in one corner.

The mood was festive and bright, and Sunny's spirits immediately lifted. This kind of community gathering was exactly the kind of small-town activity she wanted to fill her life with. As they walked toward the drink table, greeting people, she admitted that Connor's failure to attend tonight was another unmistakable sign pointing out how wrong he was for her. She wouldn't have missed this event for anything, while he obviously had no interest in being here.

Taking her new sensibleness to heart, she smiled brightly and ruthlessly shoved Connor from her thoughts.

Steve handed her a cup of orange punch. "You look happy."

"I am." She took a sip of the sweet drink. "I love these kinds of activities. Makes me feel…grounded."

He smiled over the rim of his glass, his blue eyes twinkling. "Yeah, me too. I've been coming to this thing for as long as I can remember." He nodded toward the kids carving pumpkins. "I won the carving contest a few times, too."

She broadened her smile, liking that Steve had been a part of this for so long, that he had such deep roots in this wonderful little community. Of course, Connor did, too…

She veered away from that rogue thought and refocused her attention on the here and now.

The fiddlers moved to the front of the room and then walked up the stairs to a small stage. They began another lively tune and a man's voice boomed over the public address system, announcing the first square dance of the evening.

Steve inclined his head in the direction of the dance floor. "You game?"

"You bet."

They both set their punch glasses down. Then Steve shrugged out of his jacket and put it over the back of a folding chair. He took her hand in his large calloused hand to lead her onto the dance floor. While his hand was warm and felt nice enough, she couldn't help but notice that she didn't feel the sparks she always felt when Connor touched her—

Shrill ringing cut off her thoughts. Steve stopped shy of the dance floor, muttering an oath under his breath. "Cell phone." He dropped her hand and pulled his cell phone out of his jeans pocket. He had a short, terse conversation, nodded, then hung up and turned to look at her, regret in his eyes.

"Listen, I'm sorry, but I have to go. Seth Ingersoll's prized cow, Lulabelle, is finally calving and she's had problems before. I've got to get out there right away."

"Hey, I understand," she said, her mood falling, following him to where he'd left his coat. "It's all part of the job." Even though she regretted he was leaving, the fact that he was such a valued member of this community appealed to her.

He put on his coat and then took her hand in his. "I'll try to get back, but if I don't, please enjoy yourself without me. Everybody dances with everybody, so you shouldn't have any problem finding dance partners." He leaned over and gently kissed her cheek, his whiskers rubbing her skin slightly, then pulled back and looked right into her eyes. "We'll definitely finish this date later."

She nodded, and then he turned and hurried from the room.

Sunny stood in place for a long moment, biting her lip. Steve was a nice, attractive man, probably just the kind of guy she should get to know.

But when he'd leaned close and kissed her cheek, she'd felt...well, nothing.

No sparks. No heat. None of the come-back-here-and-kiss-me-again-and-while-we're-at-it-where's-the-bedroom thoughts that had plagued her since the moment she'd laid eyes on Connor.

The ugly truth was, she was attracted to the wrong, wrong, wrong man.

Connor hung up the phone and headed toward the front door, his mother's words echoing in his mind: *Charlie Simpson's feeling light-headed. Can you come down to the festival right away and check him out?*

Connor had asked why his dad couldn't take care of Charlie since he was already there. His mom had hemmed and hawed and then finally mumbled something about his dad going to get more pumpkins from Zeb Olsen's pumpkin patch for the pumpkin-carving. Yeah, she'd made it clear Connor was needed at the festival, stat, and with someone's health on the line, he wasn't going to argue.

He grabbed his medical bag, which he kept in the closet by the door, put on a coat and left the house.

Hopefully, eighty-five-year-old Charlie's light-headedness wasn't serious. But given his family history of heart problems, Connor had to be concerned.

Because this classified as an emergency, he decided to drive into town rather than walk as he usually did. As he backed his truck around the side of the garage, he looked up, noticing that Sunny had left a light on in her room.

Sunny. Why couldn't he get her out of his mind? And why in the hell had he watched her take off for the festival earlier with Steve, her blond hair glowing like liquid gold in the dull gray light of late afternoon, wishing in some crazy corner of his mind that he was the one taking her to the dance?

He hated dances, hated the inevitable socializing and small talk associated with them. But damn if he hadn't wished that he would be the one to touch her and talk to her long into the night, her sweet smile melting his heart, her sexy scent washing over him.

As he made his way to the festival, the intermittent rain spattering his windshield, their conversation on the porch the night before ran through his head, as it had a hundred times today while he and his dad had been running errands in Portland.

The part that bothered him the most was how Sunny had said he wasn't the "smart" choice and Steve was. While he agreed with that on a practical level—they seemed all wrong for each other—on a gut, totally male level he was drawn to her. He wanted to be with her.

Too bad. He was oil, she water. They just didn't mix. Plus, she'd made it clear last night that she wasn't in-

terested. And while he had a feeling she was as attracted
to him as he was to her—she'd sure kissed him back on
the porch—she was right. Even though he was hungry
to spend some no-strings-attached time with the woman,
he had no intention of letting himself get sucked into another relationship he would fail at.

He and Sunny were going nowhere.

He pulled up in front of the community center and
parked in a No Parking zone. He grabbed his bag and
hurried in, noting that the rain had let up. He went
straight into the gathering hall. The festival was in full
swing, despite Charlie's urgent-sounding medical
"emergency."

He looked around, expecting to see a group of people clustered around a sick old man, or a pale-faced
Charlie at the very least. But he didn't see anything but
people partying.

He frowned, then scanned the room again for Charlie's snow-white head of hair. A moment later, he saw
him square dancing like a madman with Myrtle Win-
stead, who, Connor had heard, was the hot mama of the
geriatric set in Oak Valley. Go, Charlie.

Connor watched Charlie swing Myrtle around with
the energy of a sixty-year-old. Either Charlie had made
a miraculous recovery, or Connor had been set up.

He ground his back teeth together, then put himself
into motion and headed for the dessert table, which, as
usual, was his mom's domain. She had some major explaining to do.

Before he made it to the other side of the room, a

warm hand on his arm stopped him. He turned and saw Sunny standing there, looking lovely in black pants and a clingy blue sweater that accentuated her curves perfectly. She had her hair pulled up into a soft bun with a few wispy curls hanging down around her face, and her clear brown eyes made his heart pound.

"Hey, Connor." She smiled, actually looking happy to see him. "What are you doing here?"

Man, she looked good. Every time he saw her she somehow became more beautiful. As for her in that tight sweater…well, he hadn't seen anything so sexy in a long, long time. Raw desire slammed into him. "I…well, I'm looking for my mom." He glanced around. "Where's Steve? Don't tell me he left you unattended." If she were *his* date he wouldn't let her out of his sight. Ever.

She shook her head. "No, he had to leave. Emergency cow birth."

"Ah. The life of a vet," he said, surprised that he was glad Sunny and Steve wouldn't be spending the evening together after all. "I hope his emergency turns out to be real."

"Why wouldn't it be?"

"No reason. Just making a joke." He wasn't going to share with her how he'd been called here under false pretenses, especially since his mother's motivation was beginning to become clear. Sunny was obviously now dateless. His mom had spotted a meddling opportunity and had lured him here with a fake story about a sick old man, knowing Connor would rush down like a good little doctor. It looked like she'd decided to do some very clumsy, very futile matchmaking.

Just as that disturbing thought hit him, he saw The Matchmaker herself making her way toward him, waving, a broad smile of total innocence on her face.

Damn, he didn't need his mom butting in, arranging for him to ride to Sunny's rescue. And a drop-dead gorgeous woman like Sunny didn't need anybody's help—especially not his. But he wouldn't call his mom on her meddling right now, in front of Sunny. He'd do that later.

His mom arrived, a knowing look glowing in her eyes. "Connor. Sunny. I see you two found each other."

He glared at his mom. "Oh, big surprise."

"Really, Connor," she said, using what he remembered from his childhood as her scolding tone. "I have no idea what you're talking about. How lucky that you've arrived, though. Sunny is on her own now," she said, gesturing to her. "Why don't you two dance?"

His mom was a subtle as a bulldozer, but the thought of dancing with Sunny, of having a legitimate reason to touch her, had jolted its way across his mind like a defibrillator's shock more than once today. Holding Sunny close was probably the only thing that would drag him out on the dance floor.

Warming up in a hurry to the tempting idea of dancing with her, despite his dubious dance skills, he looked at Sunny. "What do you say?"

Sunny peered at him for a long moment, then turned her assessing gaze to his mom, one brow lifted. "I say it's amazing how you showed up as soon as Steve left."

His mom laughed gaily. "It is, isn't it?" she said, beaming. Jeez. What a con artist. "You two have fun." She scurried off, waving down Martha Fentner, one of her best friends, presumably to have an urgent powwow about the dessert table setup.

Connor looked at Sunny, shaking his head. "Hey, I'm sorry. She gets a little carried away sometimes."

"No need to apologize," she said, holding up a hand, her gaze moving to the medical bag in his hand. "Ah, I see." A sparkle grew in her eyes. "She got you down here under false medical pretenses, didn't she?"

"I'm afraid so, and like a total idiot, I fell for it." He rubbed his neck. "I love her, but she drives me crazy."

"No harm done, though, right?" She looked away, chewing on her lip; then she leaned close, too close, her flowery scent reaching his nose, making his blood simmer. "I mean, what's the harm in a few dances?"

He stared at her. Well, well, well. Was it possible that she wanted to dance with him as much as he wanted to dance with her? Pleasure filled him. Actually, what *was* the harm in a few dances?

He couldn't deny that being close to Sunny for the next hour was too appealing too pass up, even though he'd never learned to dance because he'd always thought square dancing was a silly waste of time. How hard could it be?

He put his medical bag down on a nearby table and took off his coat, draping it over a chair. He then turned to Sunny and held out his arm. "Let's go, then."

She grinned and grasped his upper arm from underneath, her fingers burning through his shirt like hot embers, shooting fiery sparks into his bloodstream. Suddenly, he wished they were all alone, losing themselves in hot, deep kisses and the feel of naked flesh upon naked flesh, whispering in the dark.

He swallowed hard and walked her to the dance floor, realizing way too late that dancing with her might not be so innocent after all.

Sunny held on to Connor's muscular arm, her fingers tingling, anticipating a rousing square dance experience. Before they made it to the dance floor, though, a young boy in an arm cast ran up to Connor.

"Dr. Connor," he said, his face flushed with excitement. "Can you help me carve a pumpkin? I can't carve because of this." He held up his cast-covered arm.

Connor shot her an apologetic look. "Do you mind?"

She smiled, touched that Connor would take the time to help this boy. "Of course not."

The boy skipped off, Connor in tow, towards the pumpkin-carving area. Sunny followed to watch, smiling.

After a lot of serious discussion, Connor and the boy picked out a large pumpkin from the pile. Connor hefted the thing to the newspaper-covered carving table and they both sat down, then put their heads together to carve the perfect pumpkin. They started with a crude drawing, moved on to the cutting and gut-scooping, then proceeded on to the actual carving.

Jenny walked up, a plate of finger foods held in her hands. "Hey, Sunny."

Sunny smiled at her. "Hey yourself." She returned her attention to the big man and young boy carving their pumpkin, nodding toward them. "Who's that boy?"

Jenny licked her fingers and then looked up. "Danny Jones, Edith Largo's grandson. His parents were killed in a car accident and he came to live with Edith about a year ago."

Ah, so this was the grandson Edith had been so concerned about, the boy she and Connor had discussed. "Poor kid. He and Connor seem to get along well."

"Oh, yeah. Since Danny doesn't have a dad, Connor spends a lot of time with him, mostly playing baseball—or at least until Danny broke his arm. He adores Connor."

Sunny's insides warmed, radiating a warm glow outward. "Connor likes kids?" she asked, though she shouldn't care.

"Loves them. He's a big kid at heart, and would play in the mud with them given the chance."

Astonished by this unimagined side of Connor, Sunny watched, her heart melting. Connor patiently and lovingly helped the boy, who gazed up at Connor, smiling, his eyes shining with happiness. The two of them clearly shared a touching bond, and the sight of a practical, relationship-inept Connor scooping out pumpkin innards created a tightness in her chest and almost brought tears to her eyes.

Connor and Danny finished carving the pumpkin and Connor lifted it onto the hay bales that had been set up to display the carved masterpieces. Danny nodded in approval, and then another boy approached him, waving him to the dance floor where a group of kids were dancing, leaving Connor alone.

He immediately looked at Sunny, holding out his arm, nodding in the direction of the dance floor. With anticipation and admiration and happiness bubbling through her, she walked over, placed her hand back on his firm, muscular arm, and let him lead her to the dance floor.

A few minutes later, she had to concede that Connor was the worst dancer in the place—maybe on earth.

"Connor!" she hollered over the music, waving her arms. "Allemande *left*." She gestured wildly left. "That way."

Connor looked at her, his green eyes alight with confusion, and dutifully turned around and went in the opposite direction, clumsily winding his way through the steps, almost knocking several people over.

When they met up again, he smiled sheepishly. "I didn't know this was that hard."

Before she could respond, or ask him why he didn't know how to square dance like all of the other people of Oak Valley, the caller called for a promenade right.

She stopped to grab Connor's hands, but he kept walking—right into the couple in front of them. "Connor!" she said loudly again, holding her hands out for him to take. "Promenade right!"

He said a hasty apology to the couple he'd almost mowed down, then hightailed it back to Sunny and took her hands. She pulled him along like a recalcitrant child, instructing, "We have to skip!"

He made an effort to follow her orders, but it was obvious he had no idea how to skip. He sort of loped along, throwing his feet in the air in an attempt to imitate her skipping. Before she could stop him, he got going too fast, his huge feet flailing, and kicked the round woman ahead of them right in her generous rear end.

She squealed and whipped around, her eyes seething with indignation.

Sunny pulled Connor to a stop, her eyes wide, holding in a huge laugh.

"Oh, Anne, I'm so sorry," he said to the woman. "I'm just learning."

The woman's face softened. "That's okay, Doc. Ernie here," she said, gesturing to her rotund husband, "had a hard time learning to square dance, too."

That particular song ended, and Connor turned and looked at Sunny, red-faced. "Maybe we should take a break before I hurt someone."

Sunny smiled, nodding, unable to help admiring this humble, bungling side of him. Nothing like public failure to soften a repressed perfectionist's edges and make him seem appealing. And she had to admit that she was impressed that he'd stepped on the dance floor at all. Who would have imagined that a man as muscular and athletic as Connor could be such an uncoordinated gomer?

Fanning herself against the heat generated by lots of hardworking square dancers and her grand but futile attempt to keep her inept partner on track, she said, "Sounds good." She followed him off the floor, enjoying the way his broad shoulders flowed down into a narrow waist and a tight butt. "I could use some fresh air."

"Me, too." He gestured to a side door and held out his hand. "I happen to know where that door leads. Let's go outside."

It seemed like the most natural thing in the world to take his hand and let him lead her outside. Vague alarm bells went off in the back of her mind—she wasn't supposed to be spending any time with Mr. Huge-Temptation-But-All-Wrong-For-Her.

She ignored those insistent bells, letting herself be carried along by the moment and the attractive, considerate, pumpkin-carving guy in front of her, unable to say no to him or the impetuous woman she'd repressed so much lately. Besides, she was sure sensible Connor would keep a handle on things and slide back into his practical self if necessary.

She followed him outside into the cool October evening air. Thankfully, it had stopped raining, leaving the scent of rain-washed earth behind. It was finally beginning to feel like autumn.

Connor made his way around the corner to the back of the building to a charming garden, complete with arbor, wooden bench and soft outdoor lights illuminating the stone pathway that wound through it.

He stopped and turned to look at her, his large, warm hand holding hers. "I thought you might like this spot. My mom's most recent civic contribution."

Impressed, she looked around at his mother's handiwork. Though most of the flowers and plants were fading, the trees and shrubs were still lush and green, making it a perpetually peaceful, beautiful spot. She could only imagine how wonderful it would be in full bloom on a warm summer evening, a beautiful Oregon sunset glowing in the background.

"It's lovely," she said, very aware that her hand was still in his. "Your mom's a wonderful gardener." She didn't look at him, but she could sense his eyes on her.

He remained silent, and the still, shadowy evening engulfed her. All at once, she realized how very alone they were and how incredibly aware she was of the big, masculine man standing next to her.

Looking for a distraction, she said the first thing that came to mind. "You're wonderful with Danny, you know."

He lifted one shoulder. "He's a nice kid."

"And you're a good man. He clearly adores you."

"That's because I'm the only adult male in his life."

She frowned. "Jeez, Connor. Why don't you give yourself some credit?" Without thinking, she moved closer until she was facing him, then reached out and lightly touched his chest with her free hand. "You're better with people than you think. Why can't you see that?"

He drew in a hissing breath, then reached out and touched her cheek with a fire-tipped finger. Unable to resist his pull, she looked up, right at his shadow-hidden face, and her eyes melded with his. Currents of attraction jumped in the air as she helplessly fell headfirst into his dark gaze.

A hot shudder skated up her spine and a warm, pulsing heat settled in the pit of her belly, momentarily overriding the hazy knowledge that she was wandering into dangerous territory. "I should walk away," she murmured, knowing as she spoke that something elemental was holding her there, something shared between a man and a woman she had no control over. "This is wrong."

"You might be right, but I don't want you to walk away," he said, caressing her cheek. His deep, sexy voice wrapped around her, sending more heat and sparks into her bloodstream to singe her from the inside out.

So much for Connor keeping things under control. Where was Practical Man when she needed him?

He lowered his head, his intense eyes staring into hers, clearly daring her to walk away from the heaven she would find in his arms. Daring her to walk away from a man whose tender care of a young boy had touched her deep inside, breaking down the wall she'd built around her heart one brick at a time.

Oh, sweet Lord, he was going to kiss her.

And she was going to let him.

Chapter Seven

The moment Connor's lips touched hers, Sunny was lost. He groaned low in his throat and pulled her closer, his big, hot hands smoothly caressing her waist and hips through her sweater, and showers of sizzling embers exploded inside of her, setting her ablaze. She let out a soft whimper of delight. No man had ever created the overwhelming tidal wave of pure sensation and yearning inside of her that Connor did.

More significant, though, was that, along with the most intense sexual excitement she'd ever felt, she also felt a sense of utter contentment and rightness. It fell down around her like a soft blanket, wrapping her in a warm, safe, contented glow she adored.

Right or wrong, this is where she wanted to be— close to the kind man who carved pumpkins with kids, in the steely hold of his strong arms, his large, muscular body pressed close, his mouth devouring hers.

Man and woman. Nothing more.

He slanted his lips, now holding her head steady with his hands, deepening his scorching kiss, his tongue moving slickly inside of her mouth. He tasted of peppermint and just him, and she wanted to imprint his flavor and the wondrous feeling of being exactly where she belonged in her mind forever.

He trailed hot kisses from her mouth across her cheek and down to her neck, nuzzling her there, setting fresh fires along the way, upping the tempo of the hot pulsing in her lower body. Connor might act detached most of the time, but his raging kisses were anything but. She arched her head away from him, allowing him better access to that sensitive flesh, wanting him to kiss her over every single inch of her body.

"Oh, Connor," she breathed. She was stunned but thrilled by how right, how perfect, how downright wonderful it felt to be in his arms. Her knees weakening with every second that passed, sure she'd found the one place where happiness lived, where she belonged, she whispered her thoughts to herself. "How can this be wrong?"

He froze, then very slowly dropped his hands and lifted his head from the valley of her neck. He leaned back to gaze at her, a troubled look growing in his eyes, and then shook his head. Without a word he stepped back, leaving her abandoned, the night air cold on her Connor-warmed skin.

She swayed slightly when he pulled away, her knees still weak from his kisses and his roaming hands, from how amazed she was that being close to him made her feel so perfectly complete. She looked at him, now so far away, his gaze shuttered. His withdrawal cut to the bone. It was ridiculous, but she felt the loss of his arms around her, his warmth seeping into her like the sun on a summer day, making her feel wanted for the first time.

A searing pain rose in her, along with an intense disappointment she'd never expected to experience where Connor was concerned.

With this distance between them, she'd never felt so alone, so incomplete, in her life.

Connor looked at Sunny, the word *wrong* echoing in his head like a litany. Yeah, he'd been wrong to kiss her, but had done the right thing by pulling away.

He wished he'd done the right thing and left the dance the minute he'd figured out there was no urgent medical emergency. But he'd talked himself into dancing with her just to be near her, letting his body's wants take over. Big mistake.

Not only had he been a totally uncoordinated clod on the dance floor, but he'd also been touched and impressed by her good-natured coaching and patience. All he'd been able to think about was being alone with Sunny, kissing her, holding her close.

He swiped a hand through his hair, then tilted his head to the side, trying to ease the ever-present ache in his neck. He muttered an oath under his breath, his heart twisting when he saw Sunny's slight frown and the sadness reflected in her eyes.

Damn. He'd hurt her.

But he'd had no choice. She stirred up too many frightening things in him—desire, yearning, an attraction like he'd never known—and he didn't want to deal with those things ever again.

He had to protect himself from inevitable failure and he had to protect Sunny, too. He was pretty sure she wasn't the type he could get just physical with. No, she wanted the whole happily-ever-after package—wedding, babies, lifetime commitment—and he couldn't offer her that. Hell, he wasn't even planning on staying here, the town she'd chosen to live in.

He would only hurt her in the end, and he couldn't bear that, any more than he could bear having his own heart cut out when he failed.

"Sunny, I'm sorry," he said, his voice raspy. He cleared his throat. "I shouldn't have brought you out here."

She wrapped her arms around herself, her eyes full of hurt. "Why?"

He stepped closer, wanting to take her in his arms and comfort her, but held back, unsure of his untrustworthy control around her. "We've had this discussion before."

She nodded, sighing. "I know, but…tell me again."

"Well, for starters, we want different things."

"That's true, but maybe we could keep it simple—"

"No." He emphatically shook his head and paced away. "There's no simple way with us." He was too damn attracted to everything about her to keep it simple. "Getting involved on any level would be…complicated."

"And do you avoid complication at all times?" she asked, a trace of bitterness in her voice, moving closer. "Mr. Sensible to the rescue, right?"

Her flip attitude rubbed him the wrong damn way. "*Hey*," he ground out. "Someone needs to be sensible here, one of us has to look at this realistically, and I'm good at that." He looked at her, drilling his gaze into her. "You're not."

She met his eyes with angry defiance, her chin in the air, but remained silent.

He continued. He had to lay it on the line so she would fully understand why he'd pulled away. Maybe that would ease some of her hurt. "You want someone to commit to. I don't." He took a deep breath, reached out and touched her hand lightly. "I'm not even planning on staying in Oak Valley much longer."

Her wide-eyed gaze flew to his. "You're not?"

Shaking his head, he said, "Nope. I haven't told anybody but you, not even my parents, but I'm hoping to find a job in medical research in a big city."

"But you just moved back here. Why would you want to leave so soon?"

He shrugged. "I only moved back here because I promised my parents I'd take over for my dad a long time ago, not because I really wanted to. As soon as I can find a way to swing it, I'm leaving."

She was silent for a long moment. "Okay," she finally said, her voice small. "Obviously, I had no idea about that. If that's your dream, of course you should follow it." She moved closer still and he had to clench his hands at his side to keep from reaching for her.

"But there's more to this than your leaving. Why are you so dead set against commitment?"

His insides clenched. Damn, he wished she wasn't so perceptive. The last thing he wanted to do was air his dirty romantic laundry and admit to all of his failures. But after he'd come on to her so strongly, only to abruptly back off, he owed her an explanation.

"It's pretty simple, really." He paced away, his hands shoved in his pockets, uncomfortable with opening up to her. "I've failed at every romantic relationship I've ever had. I hate failing. It doesn't take a genius to figure out how to avoid it." He left it at that. No way was he sharing with her how painful every one of his breakups had been, how his heart had bled. Some things were better left unsaid.

"So let me get this straight," she said, her voice laced with incredulity. "None of your relationships have worked out, so you've just given up on love?"

He inclined his head. "Yeah, I guess that sums it up."

She snorted under her breath, but didn't say anything.

He walked over and looked at her, his brows held high. "Do you have a problem with that?"

She turned and skewered him with her dark eyes. "Of course I do. Love's tough, I'll give you that. It can tear you up from the inside out. But avoiding it to make sure you don't fail is…well, quite frankly, it's stupid. Think what you might be missing out on."

"All I'm missing out on is a ton of pain and heart-ache. But I shouldn't be surprised you see things differently. It figures an incurable romantic like you would think that way. I see avoiding things I'm bound to fail at as just being practical."

She shook her head and rolled her eyes, a small smile on her lips. "You're impossible, you know." But then her smile faded and an almost imperceptible sadness grew in her eyes. She looked at him, lifting one slim shoulder. "I guess I didn't really realize exactly how much of a dead end you and I were."

"But you see it now, don't you?" he asked, hating that he'd had to point out the bitter truth to her. It would be wrong to let her get her hopes up for a future.

She laughed humorlessly under her breath. "Oh, yeah. Congratulations. You've done a wonderful job of convincing me how wrong we are for each other." Putting herself into motion, she moved out of the garden toward the door around the corner that led to the gathering room inside. She stopped and looked over her shoulder. "Good thing one of us is sensible, right?" she said softly. And then she continued on, her heels clicking on the concrete, leaving him alone.

He stood there without moving, his chest suddenly, amazingly, hollow and cold. His practical side screamed that he should be glad she was gone.

But another side of him, a hidden side he rarely acknowledged, told him something completely different, its tiny voice exploding inside of him like a small but deadly nuclear bomb.

You've made a massive mistake, Forbes.

He did his level best to pretend he hadn't heard that voice, *that it was wrong,* hoping the loneliness and regret burning inside of him wasn't a permanent affliction.

Because he sure didn't have the medicine for that.

Sunny returned to the festival but held herself on the sidelines for a few minutes, regaining her equilibrium, her mind bursting with what Connor had told her. She was stunned that the man was actually afraid to love because of past failure! Her heart ached at the thought of him going through life alone simply because he'd been burned before.

Despite how much she didn't want him to end up by himself, though, she had to admit he'd probably been right to put on the brakes during their searing kiss. He was leaving, for heaven's sake. That alone sealed his fate where she was concerned. Three-month trial period or not, she loved it here and would find a way to stay in Oak Valley for as long as possible, hopefully the rest of her life, fulfilling the pact and making her own dreams come true.

Even though a relationship between them was doomed for so many reasons, her chest still burned and ached with regret. Being in his arms, kissing him, had been heavenly, wonderful and exciting, light years beyond what she'd felt with any other man. She'd felt so complete, so happy. So wanted.

Well, that was too darn bad.

Going into her broken record mode, she sternly told

herself she had to keep her distance from Connor, to forget him.

Feeling hollowed out and raw, she hurried from the gathering room, needing to be by herself with her conflicting thoughts.

She went out the front door of the community center, taking a deep breath of the cool, damp evening air to clear her reeling mind, needing distance from the crowd.

She still couldn't get the sight of Connor gently helping that boy out of her mind, still couldn't forget how being in his arms, kissing him, had felt like coming home after being away for a long time. She could give herself lectures all day long about how wrong Connor was for her and vow to forget him, but the frightening truth was obvious.

None of her mental lectures would make any difference if the increasingly real, generous and kind Connor Forbes continued to shine through.

Unfortunately, he was quickly revealing the multifaceted man who was so much more than the grumpy, out-of-touch guy she'd initially thought he was.

Worse yet, he was rapidly becoming a man who could be impossible to resist.

What in the world was she going to do about that?

Rather than return home and risk encountering Sunny, Connor decided to go to his office to catch up on some paperwork and reading after the festival ended. He was having a hard time getting their sizzling kiss and the emotional conversation after it out of his mind. The last thing he wanted was to be reminded of how much he wanted to kiss her again—and that he'd be an idiot to follow through with that desire.

When he finally returned home, it was late enough that he was pretty sure she'd already be in her little room above the garage, asleep. That thought was confirmed when he exited his truck and noted that the lights above the garage were off.

He let himself into the house, trying not to think about Sunny in her bed and how much he'd like to join her there. Telling himself to cool his jets, he started up the stairs. Hearing voices in the kitchen, he turned around and made his way there to shoot the breeze with his parents for a few minutes. He was sure his mom would be full of local gossip after the biggest social event of the season, and he still needed to call her on her ridiculous matchmaking.

He walked into the kitchen and smelled herbal tea. But instead of finding his mom and dad, he saw Sunny and his mom sitting at the kitchen table, talking, with steaming cups of tea in front of them, Rufus lying at their feet. Connor's pulse jumped and memories of the way Sunny's lips had felt opening beneath his blasted into his brain. Warmth spread below his belt.

Damn, Sunny was everywhere.

And his libido was in perpetual overdrive.

His mom saw him and gave him a wan smile. "Connor. Why don't you join us?"

He moved into the kitchen, concern rising, smacking down his overactive hormones. "Mom, you don't look well." He noted her pallor. "Another migraine?"

She nodded. "They always seem to come on at the worst times, with no warning. I had to leave the festival early."

He pressed a hand to her forehead to make sure she wasn't feverish. "No fever, as usual. Have you taken the medication Dad prescribed?"

She shook her head. "You know that doesn't work for me."

He pulled his mouth into a frown, avoiding Sunny's interested tawny gaze. "Why aren't you in bed, sleeping it off like you usually do? Does Dad know what's going on?" He squinted at the bright light shining above the table. "Here, let's turn this light down."

His mom put a hand on his arm. "Connor, calm down. Sunny's taken care of me."

He stilled, his hand on the light switch. "She did?" He slowly turned and looked at Sunny, lifting a brow. "How did you do that?"

Sunny held up her hands and wiggled her fingers in the air. "I'm a massage therapist, remember?"

He pulled in his chin, skepticism running rampant. "So you *massaged* her migraine away?" He held back a *yeah, right.* Why would massage work when every other treatment his mom had tried had failed?

Sunny glared at him, fire suddenly burning in her eyes. "I've been working on some deep tissue massage techniques that have proven remarkably effective for migraines. Drugs aren't always the answer, you know."

He highly doubted a simple massage had made his mom's incredibly stubborn migraines go away when science hadn't been able to achieve that feat. "So, Mom, how do you feel?" he asked, sure she would confirm that fact.

She inclined her head. "I don't feel one hundred percent, but I do feel pretty good, considering an hour ago my head felt like it was going to explode."

He shook his head, surprised. The only explanation he could come up with was that his mom's recovery was a coincidence. But before he could corral his incredulous thoughts, Sunny spoke up.

"Don't look so darn surprised, Dr. Forbes." Her voice was soft but tinged with steel. "Nontraditional healing has been known to be effective for lots of ailments, you know. Maybe you need to move your antiquated thinking into the twenty-first century."

He clenched his jaw. It was no secret she was at the opposite end of the spectrum from him regarding healing. But he wasn't going to get into it with her over something they would never agree on.

Before he could reply, his mom stood. "I'm going to hit the hay," she said, moving toward the kitchen door. "You two go easy on each other." She left the room, a ghost of a smile on her face.

Connor rubbed his neck, easing the ache there, then turned his attention back to Sunny. "And maybe you need to give conventional medicine a little more credit," he said. "My guess is prescription drugs do far more to help migraine sufferers than massage ever will."

"You might be right," she said, rising. "I've never had a problem with the more traditional ways of healing." She walked over and looked him right in the eye. "But you need to see that sometimes nontraditional treatments like massage can work wonders." She smiled smugly, nodding toward his neck. "I could probably massage that crick out of your neck in no time. Too bad you'll never know how good that would feel."

She sauntered out of the kitchen, leaving him to wonder just how fantastic her hands would feel on his neck, rubbing the tight muscles, her touch sure and warm, gentle yet strong…

He doggedly dragged his thoughts away from a massage from the incredible Sunny Williams. It was a waste of time to torture himself with a stupid fantasy that would never come true. What was important here was that he had been confident when he'd agreed to this three-month deal of his dad's that Sunny would fail. He still didn't really believe her way of healing was particularly useful, but it was hard to argue with the success she'd had getting his mom's headache to go away. He admired Sunny for being able to help his mom when nothing else had.

He grudgingly gave Sunny some credit, even though in doing so, he was going to have a harder time getting rid of her down the line.

Worse yet, after kissing her, holding her close and feeling so damn happy around her, another ridiculous thought was taking up all the space in his brain.

He wasn't sure he wanted to get rid of her at all.

Chapter Eight

Connor left his office, his Mr. Commitment appointment an hour ago with Sam Dutton festering in his brain like an infected wound.

Bowing to local pressure, Connor had grudgingly agreed to start seeing a select few patients as Mr. Commitment, of whom Sam was the first. Sam was having problems with his girlfriend, who wanted to get married right away while Sam wanted to wait. Connor had had absolutely no idea what to tell the guy, apart from telling Sam what he would do, which, unfortunately, included his feelings on committing, or more specifically, *not committing*. Sam had left, quite clearly confused, and Connor had felt very, very inadequate.

Talk about failure.

He reluctantly pushed the door open to Sunny's office and stepped inside and was hit by the smell of the earthy-scented candle burning on the reception counter. It reminded him of the autumn days he'd spent out in the woods sketching.

He wasn't thrilled about being here, especially since he'd failed so miserably with Sam, but the buzz around town about Sunny's success in helping with a number of his patients, including his mom, had prompted him to come over and see what the big deal was.

He'd spent the past two and a half weeks successfully keeping his distance from Sunny. He left the house every evening and returned to his office or his half-renovated house, then came home late and always went straight to his room instead of stopping in the kitchen, where she and his mom usually chatted.

He hadn't been able to avoid Sunny completely at work because they were working together with several patients—her idea, not his—but he'd managed to keep those meetings brief and businesslike. He was proud of himself for that. Sunny was still the most beautiful woman he'd ever laid eyes on and her mere presence never failed to affect him physically. The last two weeks had been hell. While the woman was easing everyone else's pain, she was nothing but a literal pain in the neck to him.

Today was no exception. She looked up from behind the reception desk and smiled the bright, welcoming smile that always took him out at the knees. She was dressed in a bulky, cream-colored, cable-knit sweater and jeans that looked as sexy as hell on her.

He suppressed a groan and rubbed his aching neck, reminding himself he was here to see what all the talk was about, not drool over Sunny. Although, he couldn't really forget that he'd spent the last few weeks fantasizing about her hands on his body, stroking, rubbing, massaging…

Her smile faded and a wary light entered her eyes when she saw it was him. "Dr. Forbes," she said, all business, her chin rising. She walked out from behind the counter. "What can I do for you?"

He clenched his jaw, hating how aloof and uptight she always became when he was around. Damn it, they'd kissed, more than once, and had shared a couple of fairly intimate moments. Why did she always treat him like he was a disgusting chore she had to deal with?

Get a grip. It didn't matter how she treated him.

"I've heard from a number of my patients that you've done wonders for them," he said.

She gave him a tight smile. "That surprises you, doesn't it?"

"Sort of," he replied, nodding. "Although not really. I've seen how much your deep tissue massage has helped my mom. She hasn't had a migraine since you started." It really was amazing, considering his mom had been plagued with debilitating, weekly headaches for years.

"Well, knock me down with a feather! The great Dr. Forbes has changed his mind." She shook her head as if that was too incredible to be true, then moved back behind the counter and began to shuffle through some paperwork. "So why are you here?"

He pulled his gaze away from the tempting curves of her rear end, shown off by her snug jeans. "Uh, well…' He trailed off, suddenly feeling very foolish for showing up in the first place.

"Are you finally going to let me get rid of that crick in your neck?" she asked without looking up.

"Yes," he answered without thinking.

She glanced up with a blink of surprise, and the fact she hadn't thought him in control enough to handle a neck rub had him strengthening his answer. "Yes, if you can fit me in." He warmed to the idea. A neck massage was the perfect way to validate her success, to discover once and for all if the town was simply a victim of her warm smile and winning ways.

She pulled in her chin, furrowed her brow and then slowly pressed her mouth into a triumphant smile. "I'm sure I can." She walked back out from behind the counter, a swagger in her step. "Really, Doctor, are you sure that's a good idea, my methods being so…how did you put it?" She tapped her chin. "Useless?"

He winced inside, remembering the first conversation they'd had, how arrogantly certain he'd been that what she did had no value. Though he still wasn't completely convinced of the worth of her methods, he couldn't deny that Sunny had helped his mom. That alone earned her tons of points in his book. "You have an amazingly good memory."

"I never forget a slam," she said, staring daggers at him.

He held up his hands in mock surrender. "Hey, you caught me by surprise that day. I officially apologize for my rude behavior. You're not the only one to complain," he admitted, leaning on the counter. His lack of "interpersonal relational skills," as his last girlfriend had called it, had landed him in hot water, and had him dumped, more than once.

She looked at him for a long moment, one brow raised, and then grinned. "I have to say, apology looks good on you."

"I aim to please."

"Well, I wouldn't go that far," she said, pushing a lock of shiny hair behind one ear. "So, I gather you're in need of a little massage therapy, right?"

He pushed off from the counter, nodding, then winced when his neck spasmed, shooting pain into his upper back. "Actually, my neck's been killing me for quite a while. I might as well give your hands a shot." He gazed down at the desk, looking for her appointment book. "When can you fit me in?"

She strolled toward him, an unmistakable glint of challenge in her eyes. "How about right now?"

Surprised she had an opening so soon, given the hordes of men who'd shown up here lately, he said, "Well, uh…I don't expect you to drop everything for me." No matter what his purpose was for wanting a massage, it would still involve her touching him, and he probably needed to work up to handling that.

"Trust me, I'm not. It's my lunch hour, and someone cancelled, so I don't have another patient for a while."

He looked at his watch. "Well, I do, in fifteen minutes. It might be better if I scheduled something for another day."

"Ah. I see." She thought for a moment, a speculative expression on her face. "Why don't you have a seat here," she said, gesturing to a wheeled office chair behind the desk, "And I'll just rub your neck for a few minutes, take the edge off. Then you can make a real appointment and come back another time."

Even though what she was suggesting seemed a little more personal than what he'd had in mind, his neck was killing him. And the prospect of her hands on him was too much to pass up.

"Sounds good," he said, because, damn, it did. He moved behind the desk and lowered himself into the chair she'd indicated. She walked behind him, settling her hands on his shoulders. His body surged to life at her touch, his nerve endings sizzling, a banked fire beginning to burn within.

She began to rub his aching neck and shoulders, gently kneading his knotted muscles, her hands strong and sure and perfect. A deep, gratifying pleasure flowed through him and he let out an involuntary moan of pure relief—and arousal.

Maybe this wasn't such a good idea after all—

But before he could force any words past his suddenly dry throat, she spoke, her voice low, sexy, all Sunny. "Oh, Connor. You're nothing but knots." She pressed hard with both hands, deep into his musculature, rubbing a particularly tender spot between his neck and shoulder. Another low groan of satisfaction snuck out of him and he instantly changed his mind about whether this was a good idea or not. Anything this wonderful had to be just fine. He hazily wondered why he'd waited so long to have her do this.

She rubbed and kneaded his sore muscles for a while in silence, and he greedily sucked in the sensation of her soothing hands on him, loving every second. He could get used to this kind of treatment. Fast.

After a few minutes, she spoke. "Normally, I'd have you take off your shirt," she said, bending near, her breath whispering across his ear, her provocative scent spilling into his system like a forbidden aphrodisiac. "Too bad we don't have more time."

Hell, yes. The embers her touch had created mixed with her closeness to create an explosion of blazing fire deep in the pit of his belly, singeing his entire body. He was a man on fire.

Driven by a primitive need he'd been trying to ignore since Sunny had waltzed into his life, he turned his head and met her heated stare. He instantly drowned in the golden flecks floating in her beautiful eyes.

At that moment, with her hands on his body, her smoky gaze tangling with his, he lost all his perspective. Without really considering the consequences, he pushed on the floor with his feet, moving the wheeled chair behind the fabric screen in back of the desk, taking Sunny with him. Once hidden, he reached up and grasped the back of her head to pull her down for a kiss.

She met his kiss with a whimper of delight and an enthusiasm that blew his mind, her mouth opening, her tongue searching for his. Without breaking contact, she moved around so they were facing each other.

She wrapped her arms around his neck. He deepened the kiss, caressing her bottom and hips, then burrowing his hands under her sweater, hoping she didn't have a shirt on underneath it.

His hand encountered nothing but warm, silky skin. Smiling triumphantly, he moved his hands up her slim back and around—

"Sunny?" a female voice called from the front part of the office. Connor's blood instantly froze. It sounded an awful lot like his sister. Damn her timing.

With a muffled squeak, Sunny jumped away from him as if he had the plague.

Frantically smoothing her sweater down, she gestured for him to stay and she whipped around and went into the outer office, trying, he was sure, to look as if she hadn't been making out with him like a horny teenager.

He rubbed a hand over his face, letting out a heavy breath, wishing he had a little bit more of his usual control and practical outlook where Sunny was concerned.

But, obviously, he didn't have any of his customary common sense. After kissing her again, feeling her feminine curves and heat pressed against him, igniting his body like no other woman ever had, he wondered if his common sense about Sunny had taken a permanent leave of absence.

Her cheeks blazing, Sunny went into the outer part of the office, encountered Jenny and made a lunch date with her for the next day. She hoped it wasn't too obvious to Jenny that her brother's hands had been up Sunny's sweater, his lips devouring hers, just moments before.

Jenny left, thank heaven, and Sunny stood in the middle of the room, trying to regain her equilibrium and calm her runaway hormones.

Again, she couldn't help but be surprised by how rampantly hot Doctor Sensibility was once he got down to business. Man, the guy could kiss. The feel of his big, warm hands on her bare skin had almost sent her over the edge then and there.

She physically shook herself out of her sexual funk, needing to stay focused on her game plan, which, very unfortunately, didn't, *couldn't* include Connor. Sure, he could kiss like her hottest fantasy and he might seem like the kind of man she wanted when he was taking tender care of Danny, but he still wasn't a committing man and he was still planning on leaving. Nothing had changed, except maybe her definition of sexy.

Repeating that to herself over and over again—the nothing had changed part, not the sexy part—she forced herself to go back into the back office and face Connor.

They needed to talk. Clear the air. Find a way to keep their hands off each other.

He was still sitting in the chair, looking way too good, his brown hair tousled from her hands, his green eyes hooded, his square jaw whisker-shaded in the most masculine sort of way.

When he saw her, he pulled his mouth into a slow,

seductive smile, crooked his finger and gave her a come-on-over-here-and-let-me-set-you-on-fire look that almost singed her hair. He patted his thigh, clearly indicating for her to sit in his lap.

Her body heated and a steady, hot yearning bloomed in the pit of her belly. Oh, how she wanted to go to him and take up right where they'd left off. She'd never thought of a run-of-the-mill office chair as sexy before, but the thought of both of them on that chair, kissing, touching—

Stop it right this minute!

She stepped back and fanned her face, grappling for control. What was wrong with her, other than, of course, a raging case of the hots for the wrong man?

That thought brought her wayward sanity back. For the sake of the pact and the life she wanted with a man she could wholeheartedly commit to, and vice versa, she had to back away right now.

He stood, a strange, erotic light in his eyes. "What's the matter?" he asked, moving closer. He stopped right in front of her and caressed her jaw with his large, warm hand. "Feeling shy?"

She closed her eyes, yearning blooming inside of her, willing herself to ignore how his touch felt so right and wonderful, how being close to him completed her in a way she'd never experienced before. "No," she managed, stepping back. "We can't keep doing this, Connor. And I want you to know that *this*—" she gestured between him and her "—isn't part of the usual treatment." Heaven help her if he thought that she did this with all of her patients.

He stood there, his hand still outstretched toward her. Abruptly dropping his hand, he paced away, running a hand through his disheveled hair. He turned after a few long, silent moments, his brows knitted and his eyes troubled. "No offense, but you seemed willing enough earlier."

"You're right, I did. I was. It's just that…" She trailed off and sighed. How could she explain leading him on when she knew she shouldn't be getting physical with a man she didn't have a future with? She'd never gone for casual sex before and wasn't about to start now, no matter how much Connor turned her on.

Connor stepped closer. "Look, we're both adults. We can keep this just physical."

Maybe it was time to try to explain to him why it was so important that she find a man to commit to, why casual sex wouldn't work for her. "Did I ever tell you my parents never got married?"

He pulled in his chin. "No."

"Well, they didn't, and I've always hated that. As a child, I was so scared that since they weren't married, it would be easy for one of them to simply leave. I always felt so vulnerable and unstable." She paced away and then leaned against her desk, looking at the floor. "One time, after I'd seen my best friend's parents' wedding pictures, I asked my parents outright why they never had a wedding."

"What did they say?"

"They said that marriage was a government-mandated ceremony and didn't mean anything." She made a deprecating sound and rolled her eyes. "They tried to make me feel better by saying they'd said personal vows to each other, but that didn't mean much to me. I was a kid who wanted her parents to be married like all my friends' parents." She sucked in a huge breath, feeling the burn of tears in her eyes. "I love my parents, but we don't have the greatest relationship, and I'm convinced it's because of how much I resented their lack of commitment."

"Go on."

"There was another kid in the commune who felt the same way about his parents. We decided together that we'd grow up and commit to a loving romantic relationship like our respective parents never did." She swallowed, gearing up to tell him what she'd never shared with anyone but Robbie. "We also decided that if both of us hadn't committed by our thirtieth birthday, we'd marry each other." She couldn't bear to tell him that she's secretly loved Robbie for years and had always assumed they'd fulfill the pact by getting married to each other some day—until he married someone else.

He blinked, shock turning his eyes dark. "You're kidding."

She shook her head. "No, I'm not."

"So you're going to marry this guy?" he said, his lips barely moving, his gaze intense.

A wound deep inside of her throbbed, but it was a dull throb now, not the sharp dagger of pain she usually experienced. "No, he married someone else."

His face seem to relax. "Oh."

"Anyway, I turn thirty in a year, and I still have the pact to fulfill. I intend to commit to a man by then."

"You were just a child when you made this pact, right?"

She nodded.

"Can't you just forget about it then, especially since he's married someone else?"

"No, I can't, I won't. Not only was the pact sealed in blood, it was based on a very real desire to have a different sort of life than my parents did, a committed, stable one. Even though Robbie's already fulfilled his end, that need for commitment hasn't changed."

"So that's why you want so badly to commit?" he asked, his voice soft and surprisingly understanding. "Because your parents never did?"

She nodded. "Yes. I intend to find a good man to commit to, have a big, traditional wedding, settle down into a small-town existence, have lots of kids and live the wonderful, stable life I've always dreamed of."

He smiled, his green eyes teasing. "Sounds a little idealistic, doesn't it?"

His light tone eased her tension a bit, and he did have a point. "Of course it is." She grinned, thankful he could joke around yet still see the real her. "Consider the source."

He expression sobered. "Listen, I get why you want commitment, and you already know why I don't." A sad light grew in his eyes. "You're right. We aren't right for each other." He swung away, looking at the ceiling. "But it seems like we're fighting a losing battle. There's something…powerful between us, something we're both having a hard time walking away from."

"That's true," she said. Not only did she want to passionately attack him every time she saw him, but thinking about him with Danny, carving that pumpkin, always created a warmth inside of her that made it difficult to keep her distance. She wanted the wonderful man who'd helped that young boy. "But we have to. I've…I've never been into casual sex, and…well, that's all this could ever be."

Or was it? She had to admit, Connor had shown her an unexpected side of himself several times lately, a side that made her wonder if maybe he *was* the kind of sensitive, in-touch man she wanted. That maybe she was kidding herself thinking he wasn't.

Tentative hope came to life inside of her. She looked at him, trying to find the words to broach the subject.

But before she could, he let out a heavy breath, nodded and said, "I have to agree. This ends here and now." He smiled ruefully, his green eyes glinting. "No more kissing, right?"

She nodded solemnly, feeling foolish for letting her impetuous side take over and raise false dreams. She might have meager hope for them, but it was obvious Connor never would. "That's the way it has to be," she said, as much to herself as to him. Hoping for the impossible wasn't smart. It would only hurt more in the end.

He lifted a hand and rubbed his neck. "What about my neck? It feels better already."

"I'm glad I could help, but I don't think, under the

circumstances, that I should be…massaging you any more." Touching him would not only serve as a reminder of how unavailable he was, but it would also test her control, which had proven to be extremely untrustworthy lately.

After a long moment he said, "That should have been my line." Connor looked at his watch and pointed at the door. "Well, it's late. I guess I should be going."

Sunny followed him to the door, itching to call him back and put it all out on the table and share her hopes with him. But she wouldn't. She'd been insane to kiss him again and again, to let him under her skin. It was well past time to put her desire for Connor back where it belonged—in the realm of the impossible.

He left with a lift of his hand and a regret-tinged smile, and then Sunny was alone, with nothing to do but dwell on what she wasn't grabbing and holding on to with everything in her—a man who drew beautiful, wonderfully detailed pictures of woodland flowers and took the time to carve pumpkins with a fatherless little boy.

And somewhere deep inside, she wondered if she wasn't making a huge mistake by pushing him away.

Later that day, Connor sat in his office going over an article on new treatments for eczema he'd been meaning to read for quite a while.

After he read the same page three times and a pair of beautiful brown eyes materialized in his mind, he let out a heavy sigh, removed his reading glasses and rubbed his eyes. It was no use. He couldn't concentrate. His brain was full of one thing.

Sunny.

He leaned back in his chair, finally letting memories of their kiss and conversation have free rein over his mind after struggling to get rid of them all day long.

The massage had been pure bliss, and the kiss had, not surprisingly, nearly combusted him on the spot. Her sexy, feminine curves pressed against him; her soft, moist lips opened to him. It had all been the perfect combination of heat, sensation and blood-burning arousal. He could get used to Sunny in his arms in a hurry. Damn used to it.

While he would never be able to erase the feel, smell and heat of her from his memory, what was really sticking in his mind right now was the sheen of tears he'd seen in her eyes when she'd told him about her relationship with her parents.

That miserable look had hit him hard, landing like an unexpected left cross. Hell, she already had more friends in town than he did. It had floored him to find out that she and her parents had problems.

He felt for her. He was damn lucky to have such a good relationship with his own parents. Granted, he and his dad had had their differences lately, especially over Mr. Commitment, and his mother's well-intentioned meddling drove him insane. And while Connor had never really stopped to think about the "feeling" part of their relationship, he loved his folks and knew they loved him, period.

He ached for Sunny, not having a loving relationship with her parents. That had to be tough. Too bad her parents weren't around to work things out.

Suddenly, an idea popped into his head. He rose and began to pace, wondering if he was a fool for even considering it. He'd failed Sam Dutton. What if he failed at this, too?

But then, like magic, all of his doubts disappeared and he knew just what Sunny needed.

He picked up the phone and dialed. Before long, Sunny and her parents would be well on their way to healing their wounded relationship.

Unfortunately, he wouldn't be so lucky when it came to Sunny. Even though he had come to respect her as a healer, even though he admired her kind heart and generous soul, even though his insides twisted around and his breath left his chest every time he saw her or touched her, he still wasn't about to open himself up to the pain and heartache of another romantic failure.

And he couldn't forget that he was leaving as soon as he could. Sunny had started to put down roots and obviously had found the perfect place to live. But a small, intimate town like Oak Valley wasn't for him. No way could they make a romantic relationship work.

No, despite all of the compelling reasons he could find for wanting to be with Sunny for the rest of his life, the depressing truth was he wouldn't be having a relationship with her at all, much less the happily-ever-after one she wanted.

He didn't have it in him to be the man she needed.

Chapter Nine

Sunny breathed deeply on her walk home from work, enjoying what was sure to be one of the last days of an incredibly rare Indian summer. The leaves had already begun to turn color and fall, and even though the sun was shining from a cloudless blue sky, the air had cooled enough that in a week the rest of the leaves would be on the ground.

As she walked, she inevitably thought of her usual subject lately—Connor. Three days had passed since she'd come completely undone and kissed him in her office. Other than consulting with him on mutual patients, an increasingly common occurrence, thank heaven, she had managed to stick to her vow to keep her distance from him.

But it wasn't easy, especially after she saw him yesterday, helping a little old lady to her car, his arms laden with her bags. The elderly lady had been smiling up at him as if he were her savior; it had been all Sunny could do not to run outside and hug the man and tell him how wonderful he was.

Sunny had asked Jenny about it last night, and she'd told Sunny that Connor had been helping Mrs. Lancaster to her car every Tuesday and Thursday, her regular shopping days, since he'd arrived back home.

How sweet was that?

It had been worse when she'd taken Rufus on a walk two days ago and had seen Connor playing with Danny in the park. Enthralled, her heart tightening in her chest, she'd let her eyes linger on Connor and the boy, rough-housing in the newly fallen leaves, their laughter ringing out in the brisk autumn air. She'd almost broken down and joined in their game of tag, wanting to be part of the touching scene unfolding before her, to experience for herself this caring, warm part of Connor. But she'd stayed strong and kept walking, waving hello but nothing more.

She had to admit that Connor was turning out to be so much more than the repressed man she'd met when she'd first arrived. Oh, sure, on the surface he seemed inflexible and aloof. But she knew better now, had seen him in action with a frail old lady and a needy young boy. Connor's true self had shown through and she'd been wholly impressed and fascinated by the real man underneath the prickly, hard-edged exterior.

The truth was, she had to temper that emotion with a

gut-deep, forced practicality—she and Connor didn't have a chance. It was a kind of "look but don't touch" mentality, an attitude that had worked fairly well for the past three days to help her keep her distance from Connor.

She turned the corner to walk up the long, gravel driveway that led to the Forbeses' home, enjoying the scent of pine in the air. Fortunately, things in other parts of her life were going pretty well. Her business was starting to thrive and Connor had been very willing to refer his patients to her if need be. She was confident he would ask her to stay after the three-month trial period was up.

With a determined spring in her step, she rounded the long curve in the driveway and the house came into view.

She stopped dead, her eyebrows slamming together. A car that looked exactly like her parents' car was sitting in front of the house. Granted, their ancient Volvo wasn't exactly one of a kind, but it was an old clunker her dad refused to replace. She couldn't imagine there were any like it floating around Oak Valley.

A sinking feeling took hold of her and she considered going straight to her room above the garage so she'd have a better chance of not encountering her parents right away. But she discarded the idea, her maturity winning out. If they were here, why? Maybe they needed to dole out some "career advice." Despite their declarations of love and support, she could see the disappointment in their eyes every time she had to tell them her job wasn't working out.

She started walking again, moving up the stairs,

across the porch and into the house, having given up knocking when Sheila had said she was welcome to simply walk in anytime.

The moment she stepped in her nose twitched. She distinctly smelled her mom's patchouli perfume lingering in the air, the one and only scent Lily Williams had ever worn, her personal throwback to the Sixties. Any hope Sunny had that her parents weren't the Forbeses' visitors disappeared.

Sunny hung back for a moment, tugging on her lip with her teeth. She hated to admit it, but they were a sharp reminder of her old, unsuccessful life, even though they'd been instrumental in helping her move here.

Holding on to that positive thought, she forced herself to move toward the voices she heard in the kitchen, chiding herself. Seeing her parents was no big deal. They were her parents, after all, and she knew they loved her.

Plastering a smile on her face, she stepped into the kitchen, the Forbeses' usual gathering place. Sure enough, her parents were seated at the large kitchen table with Brady and Sheila, talking and laughing as if they'd known each other forever. All four turned and looked at her, their faces wreathed in smiles.

Sunny's stomach fell. Her parents looked really happy to see her. Guilt flared white-hot, warming her cheeks. Here she was resenting them for intruding on her life, expecting censure, and they looked ecstatic to see her.

"Mom. Dad," she said, moving forward, trying to

look relaxed and upbeat. "What are you, uh, wh…what a surprise."

Her brown eyes shining, her mom stood, smoothing down her light brown, long hair, which had looked the same for as long as Sunny could remember. She stepped forward and reached out, her plump arms pulling Sunny close. "There you are. I was beginning to worry."

Sunny hugged her back. If it wasn't disappointment, it was worry. "I'd have come home sooner if I'd known you were here," she said, knowing the statement wasn't entirely true. She'd really wanted to be flying high on unmistakable career success before she saw her parents again.

She moved toward her dad, who stood and flung his arm around her shoulders, squeezing hard.

"That's okay," he said, smiling. "We've had a great time getting to know Brady and Sheila." He unhitched his arm from her shoulders and looked down, his blue eyes inquisitive. "Brady says your business is doing well."

She headed toward the coffee pot on the counter, needing caffeine to boost her mood. "Yes, it is."

"That's great." He retook his seat. "Maybe you've finally found your niche."

Sunny bristled. Her dad might have nontraditional values about marrying the mother of his child, but the same couldn't be said about his work ethic. He excelled at what he did—*relationship counseling,* of all things—and expected the same of others. He'd never been able to hide that he wished Sunny was more successful in her chosen career.

She calmed herself, though, unwilling to be drawn

into a confrontation about her career accomplishments, or lack thereof, as was customary in the past, in front of the Forbeses.

"Yes, I guess I have, Dad."

"Good, good, and about time, too." He turned to Brady. "Sunny's had a hard time settling into her career," he said as if she weren't standing right there, listening.

Fisting her hands at her sides, a sudden rush of heat filling her chest, Sunny opened her mouth to speak.

But before she could, her mother chimed in with, "Now, Frank, you know Sunny is a tad idealistic, so it's taken her longer to find her true calling." She leaned into Sheila and stage-whispered, "She's got an impetuous streak a mile wide."

Sunny clenched her jaw. Why in heaven's name were they here? She certainly didn't need this kind of stress right now. How could a couple of relationship gurus be so clueless about communicating with their own daughter?

She swung away, her cheeks hot, her indignation rising. And ran smack dab into a solid, well-muscled wall of spicy scented male.

Connor.

She stumbled back and he caught her shoulders with his big hands, sending warmth into her blood, heating her from the inside out.

"Hey, there," he said, his deep voice rumbling. "What's your hurry?"

She froze looking up at him, her insides melting into a pool of pure yearning. Oh, she was very, very tempted to fling herself into his strong arms and beg him to just take her away from here. Sure, the people sitting across the kitchen were her parents, but they made her feel so inadequate. She needed an escape, even if it was only temporary.

But she could hardly run from the room screaming without looking like a complete nutcase. Instead, she stepped away from Connor and composed herself, trying to look calm when her parent-induced panic was threatening to swallow her whole. "Uh, no hurry," she managed to say. "My parents are here." She swung a rigid hand toward the table.

He looked past her, smiling. "Ah, yes, I know." He stepped around her, holding his hand out. "It's nice to finally meet you."

That sinking feeling grabbed hold of her again, squeezing the breath from her chest, making room for the stifling suspicions filling her from head to toe.

Her dad stood and shook Connor's hand, but Sunny barely noticed.

"How did you know they were here?" she asked, following Connor across the room, her eyes narrow.

Connor let go of her father's hand and turned around, his genial expression fading. He scrunched his eyebrows together. "What?"

She stepped nearer, her hands fisted on her hips, glaring up into his eyes. "I said, how did you know they were here?"

He blinked.

Before he could answer her mom piped in. "Why, because he's the one who invited us to come."

Sunny let her jaw drop, the sinking feeling hitting rock bottom and exploding like a bomb inside of her. Clenching her back molars together so hard she swore they almost cracked, she grabbed Connor by the arm and yanked on it, muttering under her breath, "I need to talk to you." She jerked a stiff thumb over her shoulder in the direction of the front of the house. "Out there."

Sensing four sets of eyes staring at her, she threw the interested parental quartet a manufactured smile. "I need to yell at—er, I need to…talk to Connor." She pulled him toward the kitchen doorway, her mouth still pressed into what she hoped was a believable smile, despite the anger roiling around inside of her like acid. "We'll be right back."

She followed him out into the foyer, gearing up to roast him. Questions bounced around in her mind. What possible reason could he have had for inviting her parents here?

She had no idea, but she'd find out and call him on it. And then she'd be smart and do what she should have done weeks ago.

Forget him once and for all.

Connor dutifully trudged into the foyer, Sunny bringing up the rear like an uptight army general, smoke surely blasting from her head.

Obviously, she was livid.

Big surprise. He'd blown it, done the totally wrong thing by inviting her parents here, just as he'd screwed up giving Sam Dutton advice. He'd been stupid to think he could be Mr. Commitment and help fix Sunny's relationship problems. Hell. Now she was probably going to have him drawn and quartered.

He reached the middle of the entryway and slowly turned around, steeling himself for her inevitable tirade.

Sunny marched toward him, her pert chin held stiffly in the air, and delivered the expected reaction right on cue. "Why in the world did you invite my parents here?" she demanded in a low voice, her hands fisted rigidly on her hips, her pretty brown eyes blazing tawny fire.

"I honestly thought I was doing you a favor."

Her face twisted. "A favor? Why would you think that?" She swung around, waving her hands in the air. "I opened up and told you about my…problems with my parents, which is a painful subject. And what did you do? As soon as I saw the sensitive side of you, as soon as I'd begun to trust you and have faith in you to share personal things with you? You went ahead anyway and invited them here, and they came—did you see what they did? Talking about me, criticizing me, and I can just see how disappointed they are—"

He grabbed her taut hands as she swept by, cutting her off, loving the feel of her soft, small hands in his, hating that he'd upset her. "Hey, would you calm down and let me explain?" He rubbed her hands. "You're as stiff as a board."

Wide-eyed, she hesitated, took a deep breath and nodded, relaxing her hands slightly.

"After we talked, I thought about what you said, and it…bothered me."

She drew in her chin at that comment, a skeptical light flashing in her eyes, but she remained silent.

He plunged on. "I thought about my relationship with my parents and how much it means to me and I guess I wanted the same thing for you." He squeezed her hands. "I thought I was helping you."

She stared up at him, her eyes searching his face and her hands tightening. With a muttered oath, she yanked away from him and paced away, her head bent. "I appreciate what you tried to do and I don't like saying this, but I have to." She turned back around and pierced him with a steely look. "Connor, you shouldn't have meddled like this. It's one thing to offer advice, but to force an issue like you did is wrong. You should have discussed this with me before you plowed ahead and brought them here."

Her words landed like stones inside of him. "I thought I was doing the right thing, that I actually knew how to fix your life for the better." Huge mistake. He should have known better than to try to be Mr. Commitment—to anyone.

"But you weren't. I'm trying to build a new life, and my parents are just a difficult reminder of the old one. I don't want them here right now."

He tightened his jaw. No way was he going to stay quiet about this. "That's bull. Have you ever actually told them how you feel? I may not know much about relationships, but even someone as backward as me can see that you need to talk to your parents and deal with this." He gestured to her. "Look at you. You're a rigid, tense mess just talking about this."

She shook her head, a shadow growing in her eyes. "No, I haven't. They wouldn't understand."

"How do you know they wouldn't understand?"

"I just do. They think their lifestyle is perfect, they always have. Nothing I say is going to make a difference."

"Maybe you should give them a chance."

"Maybe you should listen to yourself," she said, lifting a brow. "Maybe you should tell your parents that you want to be a medical researcher instead of pretending to be something you're not, instead of assuming they won't support you."

"That's apples and oranges, and this isn't about me," he said. "But for the record, I haven't talked to my parents yet because taking over my dad's practice is about honoring the deal we made and repaying my father for helping me in the past." He paused. "This is about you not wanting to take a chance to save your relationship with your parents." He put his hands on her narrow shoulders. "Geez, Sunny, don't you miss them?"

She looked stricken. "Of course I do," she said, her voice shaky. "They're my parents, and despite our problems, I love them." She pulled away, a deep, soul-searing ache visible in her eyes. "But I can't help the way I feel. I don't know how to get rid of that. I hate to disappoint them and want to make them proud. I can't do that until my business is a success."

The pain in her eyes made his chest twist. He wanted with everything in him to make her hurt go away. "Look, I'm a pretty smart guy about a lot of things, and my gut instinct is telling me that you and your parents need to talk and work this out. Don't run away from the chance to mend your relationship with them. Maybe you should try to look at the situation from a neutral, more objective perspective."

She shook her head and gave a delicate snort. "You need to take your own advice, Connor. You're doing the same thing."

"No, I'm not. I have a great relationship with my parents—"

She stopped him by holding a stiff hand in the air. "Okay, okay, except for not letting them in on your plans, I guess you do. I'm talking about you avoiding love so you won't fail."

He stilled, shocked that she'd brought that subject up and surprised that she remembered what he'd said. "That's…different."

"No, it's not. It's exactly the same. You're staying away from love and commitment—running away, actually—sure it will lead to pain and failure. You should take your own advice and quit running." She looked right at him, her beautiful brown eyes drilling deep into his. "You never know what you might find."

He returned her gaze, unable to look away from her probing stare. "What are you saying?" he asked, his voice suddenly hoarse, his mind rife with what she might be implying. "Are you talking about…us? What am I supposed to find?"

A sad light grew in her eyes and she looked away, smiling ruefully, shaking her head slightly. "You're going to have to figure that out on your own," she said.

"In the meantime, please stay out of my personal life, all right?"

With that barbed comment zinging its way into his heart like a fire-tipped arrow, she headed back into the kitchen, leaving him alone, his chest suddenly burning.

Even worse, he couldn't help but think that he was missing something very important.

Nothing new there. He was a complete relationship idiot. He'd screwed up again, committed a blatant Mr. Commitment blunder and driven Sunny away.

Surprisingly, that thought cut deep.

Much, much deeper than he'd ever expected.

Chapter Ten

Sunny remained quiet the rest of the evening, through a delicious steak dinner and scrumptious apple pie dessert. Connor's penetrating green gaze shot its way across the dining room table, wreaking havoc with her nerves and conscience. She felt incredibly guilty about rudely telling him to butt out, especially since his concern for her seemed genuine. But, at the time, genuine concern or not, she'd felt like he'd deserved it for meddling in her personal life.

Now she was having second thoughts about coming down on him so hard.

She did her best to ignore his piercing looks, focusing instead on what he'd said about her relationship with her parents, giving his advice a chance, trying to see things from a neutral perspective as he'd suggested.

Surprisingly, when she looked at the situation with her parents from an objective viewpoint—or, at least, as objective as she could be—she had to admit that Connor's advice made sense. Was it possible he knew what he was talking about?

Discussing this with them might not do a bit of good, considering her parents were good at fixing other people's relationships but had always been remarkably thickheaded about their own. No matter what the outcome, though, now that she'd calmed down, she was mature enough to concede that she and her parents needed to at least attempt to clear the air. Amazingly, she had Connor to thank for that realization.

With that in mind, after she helped Brady and Connor with the dishes, intensely aware of Connor's silent, almost remote, presence next to her, she asked her parents to join her on the porch to talk.

They looked surprised, but agreed, following her outside into the cool autumn evening.

"What's this all about?" her dad asked, lowering himself into the porch swing. "Problems with the job?"

Sunny bit her tongue, taking the mature thing to heart and cutting off a reply that involved asking why in the world he was always so obsessed with her career success. She needed to deal with one problem at a time. "No, Dad, that's going just fine," she said in all honesty, proud that, for once, she could say that and mean it.

Her mother sat down in the swing, too. "What did you need to talk about, dear?"

Sunny settled back against the porch railing and took

a deep breath, searching for a tactful way to broach the subject of her resenting their lack of commitment. Deciding there was no way to be truly diplomatic about such a personal, sensitive subject, she blurted, "Why didn't you two ever get married?"

Both her mother and father stared up at her, their jaws slack. "Ex…excuse me?" her mother said, blinking owlishly.

"It's a basic question," Sunny snapped, letting her negative mood get the best of her. "You shouldn't have that much trouble answering, or be that surprised that I'm asking."

"Actually," her dad said, "I'm surprised you didn't ask again, when you were older than a starry-eyed girl of ten, hung up on weddings and the like."

Sunny widened her eyes. Not only was she surprised he remembered that she'd asked before, she'd always assumed their lack of commitment was a nonissue to them, a lifestyle they never questioned. "You are?"

He nodded. "We've lived an…unconventional life by most people's standards. It's only natural you'd wonder why."

Sunny shifted gears. "Okay, I'm asking again. Why didn't you ever marry? And don't give me some propaganda about government-mandated ceremonies. I want the genuine, from-the-heart reason."

After a long silence, her mom spoke up. "I guess we never felt the need to. We love each other. That's what's important, right?"

"I expected that kind of rationale," Sunny muttered,

shaking her head. She moved closer, looking right at them to emphasize her point. "Did it ever occur to you that having parents who were married, *committed,* might be important to *me?*" Sudden hot tears stung the backs of her eyes. Oh, great. She did not want to cry about this.

Her mom reached out and squeezed Sunny's hand, her face soft and understanding. "Of course we thought about that, sweetheart. But we always believed that having two parents who loved each other by deed and example made up for an official document."

Sunny shook her head, biting her lip. "That wasn't enough for me. I was always so afraid that since you weren't married, it would be easier for one of you to walk away." She took a deep shuddering breath. "You guys separated three times."

"We didn't really separate," her father said. "Those were planned relationship sabbaticals, designed to strengthen our relationship."

She stared at her dad. "You never told me that. I thought you left because you were having problems."

Her mom stepped forward, her eyes soft. "In hindsight, we probably should have told you, but at the time we thought you were too young to understand anything about adult relationships."

"I thought you were breaking up," Sunny whispered, the pain she felt every time her dad had left searing her heart.

"But we didn't break up, did we?" her father said, his voice gentle and solemn. "And we're still here, together."

"But you could have easily ended the relationship,"

Sunny pointed out. "There was nothing holding you there, no tangible commitment to encourage you to stay." A familiar ache built in her chest. "I always felt so vulnerable."

Her mother stood and took Sunny's shoulders in her hands, giving her a gentle shake. "Sunny, listen to me. I'm sorry we didn't clue into how you were feeling. But you have to realize that there *was* something holding us there—you, of course, and our deep love for each other. Period. That's all, but it's huge and more than enough—it always has been. Just because we never married doesn't mean we were never committed. We've lived a loving, monogamous lifestyle that speaks for itself." She smiled, then turned her warm gaze to Sunny's father, a deep, abiding love shining in her eyes. "I still love him as much as I did thirty years ago. Maybe more. That's what matters to me, what holds me by his side, not some piece of paper saying we're married."

Sunny thought about what her mom had said, trying to take Connor's advice and look at her parents' relationship from a new perspective. She couldn't deny her mom and dad had always been inseparable, almost to the point of silliness. And she had to admit they had, by example, taught her about love…oh, heavens, and about commitment, too, she belatedly realized, shock rolling through her. In reality, they *could* have walked away at any time…but, more important, *they hadn't.*

Their love had held them together, not a marriage certificate.

That was a huge discovery for her, one that seemed

simple but wasn't. She wished she'd figured this out a long time ago, saving her the pain of always resenting her parents' seeming lack of commitment.

She shook her head, then smiled ruefully at her parents. "I've been stupid."

"No, we've been the stupid ones," her dad said, his eyes full of regret. "We should have paid more attention to how our lifestyle affected you, should have talked about this more." He looked at her, a shrewd expression on his face. "You've been avoiding us because of this, haven't you?"

She nodded, looking at the floor, ashamed that she'd let this come between her and her parents for so long, that she hadn't been able to figure out the solution on her own. "I was looking at the situation from the wrong perspective, believing the only way to gauge commitment was through a marriage certificate, instead of letting your track record speak for itself."

Her mom stood again. "Are you willing to do that now? Are you okay with this?"

"Yes," she said, her mind moving forward. She was glad they'd talked about how she felt about her parents' unconventional relationship, happy they'd worked out that problem. But there was more. As long as it was truth time, she had to confront them about how she'd felt so much pressure from them to have a successful career.

"One more thing," she said. "I know you've been disappointed about my lack of career success—"

"Hold it," her dad said, his brows scrunched together. "What do you mean, disappointed?"

She let out a low laugh. "It's no secret how much you want me to succeed. Since I haven't, you're disappointed."

Her dad came over and took her hands. "I can see we handled this badly, too. I have never been disappointed in you, honey. Just concerned that you find a job you love as much as we love ours."

She pulled in her chin. "Really? Because it came across as disappointment."

"And we're sorry for that, honey," her mom said, coming over to stand beside her dad. "We only want you to be happy."

Sunny sat back, again trying to look at this from their viewpoint, without the blinders she'd had on for a very long time. From this new perspective she could see that they really did have her best interests at heart. She'd interpreted their actions all wrong. Again.

"I misread your concern as pushiness," she said, ashamed she hadn't given them more credit. "I guess I just want to be as successful as you are."

"And it looks like you're well on your way," her dad said, pride shining in his eyes. "We're proud of you, Sunny. Damn proud."

Her eyes burned and she blinked rapidly, thankful they were tears of happiness.

"Even though this new attitude is going to take some getting used to, I feel like a huge weight has been lifted off my shoulders," Sunny said, smiling despite the tears in her eyes. "Can you forgive me for being so foolish?"

Her dad rose. "Feelings are feelings, no matter how

foolish they may seem." He pulled her to him, wrapping her in a bear hug, the scent of his aftershave surrounding her, somehow wrapping her in a sense of security she hadn't felt for a very long time. "There's nothing to forgive. I'm just glad we got all of this out in the open." He pulled back and looked down at her. "Are you being just as foolish about Connor?"

She froze, floored by her father's ability to see that she and Connor had more than just a business relationship, despite her unsuccessful efforts to the contrary. She sidled away, looking at them from the corner of her eye. "Um…what do you mean?"

Her mom stepped forward, a knowing look in her eyes. "What he means is, are you viewing Connor from the wrong perspective, too?"

Sunny pulled her eyebrows together and took her mom's place on the porch swing, trying to look casual. "Why does how I view Connor make any difference?"

"Because you're in love with him, silly," her mom announced as if Sunny had the words tattooed on her forehead for all the world to see. "Why else?"

Sunny shot to her feet, her face blazing, intending to deny that fact with her last breath, if need be. "I don't love Connor," she said vehemently. "He's all wrong for me, definitely not the man I'm looking for. He's repressed. Insanely practical. Uptight. Clueless about love. Commitment-phobic." She crossed her arms over her chest and shook her head. "No way."

Her mom looked at her father. "Wrong perspective," they said in unison, nodding.

Sunny looked back and forth between them. "Okay, care to fill me in?"

"Of course," her mom said. "It's just this—you're focusing on the negative, rather than the positive."

A hot chill swept up Sunny's spine and her knees went weak. She leaned against the railing for support, her throat tight, unable to conjure up a response to her mother's incredibly illuminating statement.

Connor's arrival on the porch precluded her from saying anything and stopped her amazing thoughts in their tracks.

"Just passing through," he said, shrugging into his leather jacket. "Don't mind me."

"Where you off to?" her dad asked.

"I promised I'd help a young friend with some complicated math homework." He glanced at his watch. "I'm due in five minutes." He waved as he walked down the porch stairs. "Bye."

Sunny watched him walk away, unable to take her eyes off him, admiring his tall, masculine frame, her world suddenly spinning the wrong way.

He was going to help Danny with his math.

A rush of soul-searing awe and deep, intense admiration swept through her, pulling her chest tight, scattering hot goose bumps across her skin. The truth dawned on her in a blazing rush.

Her parents were right. She *had* been looking at Connor from the wrong perspective—the negative one. She'd focused so intently on all the reasons he wasn't right for her that she hadn't been able to see all the reasons he was exactly the man she was look-ing for.

She loved how he helped Mrs. Lancaster every Tues-day and Thursday without fail, carrying her grocery bags to her car, not to mention how he took care of all of his patients with true concern and commitment. She loved how he took the time to help Danny, going out of his way to make the boy feel special. She loved his sen-sitive, artistic side, the part of him that not only gave him the talent to draw such wonderful, detailed pictures but also made him want to use that talent to create things of beauty. She loved how he had such a close relation-ship with his parents and the rest of his family.

She loved Connor Forbes.

Feeling shaky at her discovery, she looked at her par-ents. "You guys are a lot smarter than I thought."

Her mom inclined her head. "While I appreciate the compliment, we can't take too much credit. It wasn't difficult to see how much you and Connor care about each other."

A bright sense of elation shot through Sunny and her hopes soared. Connor returning her feelings would be a dream come true—the perfect man to love. Him lov-ing her back—

Her hopes thudded to earth. She couldn't forget that Connor had his own reasons to not love her, reasons he obviously believed in wholeheartedly. "I'm not sure you've pegged Connor's feelings correctly," she said, vividly remembering how adamant he was about avoid-ing failing at love. "He's not particularly hot on love and commitment." She smiled wryly, rolling her eyes. "He avoids both like the plague."

"Well, you'll just have to change his mind, then, won't you," her dad said authoritatively, as if simply saying the words would make them come true.

"I wish it would be that easy," Sunny said, shaking her head, a sense of doom coming over her. "But I have a gut feeling it won't be. Connor is dead set against ever falling in love. I'm not sure I'll be able to convince him otherwise, and I'm not sure I'm up to being rejected." Connor walking away from her, throwing her love back in her face, would rip her heart out in one fell swoop.

Her mom stepped forward and placed her hand on Sunny's forearm. "Haven't you learned anything tonight?"

Sunny thought about what her mom was driving at, recalling how she'd misjudged her parents lack of commitment and how their talking about it cleared the air and helped them all gain new, healing understanding. A gut-level understanding materialized inside her, her mom's point dawning on her like the sun shining over the horizon, one beam at a time. "I need to give him a chance, talk to him about this, don't I? I can't walk away without trying, right?"

Her mom nodded sagely, eyes sparkling. "That's right."

Her parents hugged her, said good-night and went inside, leaving Sunny alone, her brain bursting with a multitude of emotions. Happiness. Relief. Intense fear.

She laughed humorlessly under her breath. She might have had a breakthrough of sorts and discovered she loved Connor. She might have figured out theoretically what she needed to do to snag the man of her dreams. But the truth was all of that was a simple, safe prelude to the frightening thing she had to do to make her dreams come true.

Risk her heart and soul for a man who might not love her back.

Chapter Eleven

Connor sat behind the desk in his father's study, looking at the letter that had arrived yesterday after Sunny had so vehemently called him on bringing her parents to Oak Valley. Her hauling him over the coals was a stinging but much-needed reminder that he still didn't have a damn clue about personal relationships.

The surprising correspondence in his hand was from his former boss, John MacDermott, the brilliant attending physician who had run Connor's butt into the ground during his residency and who now oversaw Oracle Medical Research. John had gotten wind of Connor's career aspirations through the tentative feelers Connor had put out via old colleagues and was offering him a position, effective immediately, as a medical research supervisor at Oracle's San Francisco office.

Granted, the offer had come sooner than Connor would have liked, before he'd been ready to approach his parents about what he really wanted to do. But the point was, the tempting offer *had* come and he couldn't ignore it.

Nor had he been able to ignore Sunny's advice when it had rung in his head.

Maybe you should tell your parents that you want to be a medical researcher instead of pretending to be something you're not, instead of assuming they won't support you.

Acknowledging she was right—wasn't she always?—he'd summoned up his courage and talked with his mom and dad an hour ago, telling them of his dream and the unexpected offer that he'd received.

Of course, they'd been wonderfully supportive, wanting his happiness above all else. A deep sense of shame nagged at him again. He should have known his parents would have supported him on this instead of doubting them.

Everything had fallen into place; his dream was right there for the taking. It was time to leave Oak Valley behind. He should be thrilled.

Instead, unease rolled through him like an intense summer thunderstorm, setting him on edge. Leaving Oak Valley would mean leaving Sunny, too.

Why did that bother him so much, creating a dull ache in the middle of his chest he hadn't been able to get rid of? No matter how many times he reminded himself that not only was his dream within his reach, but that he'd never wanted Sunny to be part of his life, anyway, he still couldn't fill up the hole forming in his chest.

Be practical, Forbes. This job offer was the best thing that could have happened to him.

Wasn't it?

He ran a hand over his face, hating that he was so mixed up about something that should be easy to figure out.

"Connor, can we talk?" He turned to see the object of his conflicted thoughts standing in the doorway, looking beautiful in a pair of faded jeans that emphasized her lean but feminine curves and a red, long-sleeved sweater that brought out the faint strawberry highlights in her hair. She had her plump bottom lip clamped between her teeth and looked…nervous?

Strangely, his first instinct was to take her in his arms, bury his nose in her hair, then work his way down to her delectable mouth for a soul-searing kiss. His chest twisted. Not a good idea. Rather than kissing Sunny, he was going to have to tell her that he was leaving. He owed her that much, especially since she had been instrumental in showing him that it was time for him to come clean with his parents, clearing the way for him to follow his dream and leave.

He motioned for her to come in.

She hesitantly moved toward the leather upholstered chair next to the desk and lowered herself into it, her back ramrod straight. Her eyes were filled with a strange, anxious light he couldn't make sense of.

"What's up?" he asked, fingering the letter on the desk, putting off dropping his bomb.

She looked beyond his shoulder. "I…uh, I have something to tell you," she said in a small voice. She swallowed heavily, her jumpy gaze straying to the letter he held and then holding steadily on his face. "What's that?"

He hesitated, looking at the desk, away from her curious stare. Okay. She'd opened the door. He had to walk through, even though the prospect of actually telling her, *right now,* felt like a bad case of the stomach flu. "It's a job offer."

She pulled in her chin. "From who?"

"A former boss. He wants me to come work with him in San Francisco."

Her eyes shifted away from him briefly and then she sucked in a deep breath. Her mouth quivering, she smiled. "This is what you've been waiting for, right?"

He nodded. "Yes, it is."

"You're going to accept, then?" she asked, her voice tight.

His insides burned, but he forced himself to say the words. "I am."

"So you'll be leaving?"

"Yes," he managed, amazed at how the thought of walking away from Sunny nearly killed him.

She sat silently, her face devoid of expression. Then she reached over and put her hand on his.

At her touch, warmth zinged its way into his heart.

"I know this is your dream," she said quietly. "What will make you happy. That's the most important thing to me." She lifted her beautiful brown eyes and stared at him, rising. "Congratulations." She removed her hand and moved toward the door, about, he was sure, to walk right out of his life forever.

Panic gushed into him. "Sunny, wait," he said, alarm bells going off in his head. Something wasn't right. Sunny was too damn subdued; her usual, wonderful energy was masked by a strange pall he didn't understand.

He stood, an odd sense of urgency filtering into him, mixing with his aching heart, making him feel off balance and worried. The vibes floating around the room just didn't seem right. "You said you had something to tell me."

She stopped by the door, then turned her head and looked right at him. Her eyes held an odd sadness that made his chest tight. "Oh…it's nothing important."

He walked quickly toward her, outright concern spurring him on. "Are you sure?" He touched her cheek, loving the softness and warmth of her skin. "You seem…sad."

She drew in a deep, shuddering breath, turning her head to nuzzle his hand for a heart-stopping moment. "I…guess I was just hoping you'd stay."

Her words of hope created an ache in the pit of his belly that burned him from the inside out. "I can't. I don't belong here, and I certainly don't have any business being Mr. Commitment." He paced away, shoving his hands into his pockets. "Inviting your parents here proved that, didn't it?"

She followed him, tugging on his elbow. "No," she said. "You're wrong. I was wrong. My parents and I talked last night and worked out our problems, thanks to you. You knew exactly what you needed to do and did it, the perfect Mr. Commitment response."

He stared at her, shaking his head, wanting to believe her but unable to ignore the bitter truth. "Lucky guess, that's all. I don't have a clue about relationships, I never have." He laughed humorlessly under his breath. "I haven't failed in every romantic relationship I've ever had for nothing."

"Yes, you do have a clue. I see it every day. You help a little old lady to her car, earning her gratitude and respect, and you spend time with Danny, who adores you. You draw those wonderful pictures—"

"Whoa, whoa," he said, cutting her off. "How do you know about those?"

"I saw them hanging in your mom's kitchen and asked her about them. You're very talented, you know."

He remained silent for a moment, stunned that she knew about his artwork. Being an artist wasn't something he'd shared with anyone outside of his family. "They're just charcoal drawings. Nothing special."

"They're special because you drew them. You're a wonderful artist, and you know a lot more about relationships than you think, Connor. I heard from Edith Largo, who lives next door to Sam Dutton, that he was very impressed with your advice, that you put things in perspective for him, showing him that he isn't ready to commit to his girlfriend." She put her hand on his forearm, her touch searing his skin through his cotton shirt. "Don't sell yourself short. Give Mr. Commitment a chance."

Surprised that he'd helped Sam, Connor looked at her small hand on his arm, wanting to take it and pull her into his arms and hold her forever. Wanting to believe her with everything in him.

But he couldn't believe her—it was probably just dumb luck that he'd helped Sam—and he couldn't ask for anything from her. Not now. She was staying. He had to leave Oak Valley, a place where he'd never really fit in, and follow his dream, just as Sunny had followed her dream and come to Oak Valley. She'd come, he had to leave. That was the way it had to be.

Filled with a bone-deep ache he doubted would ever go away, he took her hand in his and raised it to his lips. He kissed the soft skin, inhaling her scent, imprinting it on his mind forever.

She stared at him, her gaze intense and her eyes bright. "This *is* what you want, right?"

Doubt slapped at him from all angles. If he walked away, that would be it. There would be no coming back. No life with Sunny. Ever. He had no doubt she would move on and fulfill the pact with her perfect man, some guy lucky enough to be loved by an incredible woman like her.

For a long moment, panic and searing jealously filled him. He wished he could claim this amazing woman for his own and live the rest of his days with her. But that was just a fantasy, not something he could ever really do. He was a good doctor but a lousy romantic partner. He had to stick to what he wouldn't fail at. A failure would not only bring him to his knees, it would hurt

Sunny in the end, and that was something that would cut him to the core.

He nodded, a small movement of his head, the truth swallowing his heart whole. "It is."

She blinked quickly, her eyes shimmering with moisture, her mouth pressed into a tight line. "That's what I thought." She quickly stepped back and headed toward the door. "Good luck in your new job," she said, her voice cracking on the last word.

His instinct was to call her back. But he didn't. Couldn't. Not when there were so many reasons to let her go.

And then she was gone.

And he was alone, just the way he wanted to be, free to pursue his new job in a new city, a fresh life at his fingertips, his dream about to be fully realized.

He should be happy. But, strangely, he wasn't. Instead, a dull, cold emptiness grew inside of him, cutting off his breath and echoing with icy doubt.

He dropped into the desk chair. Everything he'd believed about himself was swirling around inside of him, mixed up and unrecognizable. Through the mess, one sweet, supportive voice stood out.

You know a lot more about relationships than you think, Connor.

Her stunning words echoed like a litany inside his reeling brain. They forced him to reexamine his own beliefs about himself, to look deep inside for the first time and really *see* his true self, warts and all.

One thing was clear. He had a lot of warts. And

Sunny had been right. He *was* running away from love and had taken the easy, safe route by convincing himself he was bad at love rather than risk failing. He hadn't had one ounce of Sunny's courage—the courage that had brought her here after failing so miserably in San Francisco, the courage that had pushed her to follow her dream, no matter that she might fail.

Suddenly, one undeniable truth crashed into his dazed brain. Wouldn't it be the ultimate failure to let his fear of commitment and failing make him walk away—from the woman he loved?

Oh, man, oh, man. Why had it taken him so long to see it? He loved Sunny with everything he had. She was kind, funny, tenacious and beautiful, and there was no way he could leave her behind.

Even though he wanted to kick himself for taking so long to figure things out, a strange sense of calm came over him. What mattered now was that he'd finally caught a clue. Even though loving Sunny scared him to death, it was a real, deep, true emotion he couldn't ignore or pretend didn't exist just to keep himself safe. The thought of being alone in a lab seemed cold and unfulfilling compared to spending his life with Sunny.

An image of that lab materialized in his brain and suddenly it didn't look as good as it once had. He'd come to this town because he'd felt obligated, not because he wanted to. But he had to admit, that after a day spent doctoring the townsfolk of Oak Valley, he felt really good.

He sagged back in his chair, floored by his two discoveries. He loved Sunny. He had actually come to like his job here. That could only mean one thing.

He stood, wanting to run to her and sweep her into his arms and shout to the world how much he loved her, that he was staying. But he stopped, insidious doubt clawing at him again, cutting into his newly discovered feelings like a razor, leaving him bleeding on the inside.

What if she didn't love him? What if he still wasn't the man she wanted? He sat back down, his menacing uncertainty eating away at him, slashing his confidence and resolve into ribbons.

What if he failed now, after he'd figured out how much he loved Sunny? Damn it all, he couldn't take the pain of losing her.

He sat, thinking, recalling another of Sunny's prophetic statements, something he hadn't understood until this very moment.

You never know what you might find.

Had she been referring to the fact that if he stopped running long enough, he would find that she loved him, too?

A chill marched up his spine. He needed to find out. And he couldn't deny that he would lose her for sure if he didn't fight for her. He had to take the risk. Good or bad, he had to tell Sunny how he felt.

Even though he might be setting himself up to get booted in the teeth again, he'd never know unless he tried.

He prayed he wasn't being a total, lovesick fool all over again.

The next day, Sunny emerged from her apartment, her eyes scratchy and puffy, her daylong crying and wallowing jag over—for now. Even though her heart was in tatters, she was determined to get on with her life and not let Connor's decision to leave Oak Valley keep her from fulfilling her own dreams. Her holistic practice would never succeed if she didn't stay on top of the paperwork.

As she walked downtown with her hood pulled up over her hair, the gray, drizzly day perfectly reflected her mood. She reiterated to herself that she'd done the right thing by holding back her feelings yesterday in Connor's dad's study, the only thing she could have done under the grim circumstances.

Even though she'd intended to tell Connor that she loved him, it was that very emotion that had kept her from actually revealing her true feelings. She loved him too much to ever make him choose between her and his dream. She couldn't go through life wondering if he would eventually resent her for forcing him to make that kind of difficult choice. She'd rather walk away, even though the thought of losing Connor made her heart weep.

And so she'd left him sitting alone, none the wiser, even though putting his needs first had left a wound on her soul she didn't think would ever go away.

Now it was time to move on as best she could, if that was possible, and immerse herself in what would help her get through this incredibly heart-wrenching event. Her work.

She walked quickly, the cold drizzle making her nose and cheeks as numb as the empty space in her chest, forcing herself to focus on anything but the incredibly sad thoughts about how she was going to get over losing the man she loved.

She approached her office from the boardwalk on the opposite side of the street and then crossed the deserted, rain-slicked pavement. She frowned when she saw Connor's truck parked in front of his office. Darn. Had her overzealous emotions fried her brain? Why hadn't it occurred to her that he might be here, too?

She kept walking, her stomach coiling. She wanted to distract herself with work, but her emotions were too raw to deal with encountering Connor just yet. She looked at his office, drawing her eyebrows together at the sight of his office window covered in paper.

Oh, no, this was too much. Of course, he was packing up, preparing to leave. Getting ready to walk out of her life.

Her heart shriveled all over again.

She stopped on the boardwalk in front of his office, tears rising in her eyes. She made herself take a long, hard look at the covered windows, forced herself to accept that Connor didn't love her and that she loved him enough to let him go. Maybe it was better this way, seeing the unmistakable sign of his intention to make a new life somewhere else—without her.

She stood there for a long time, the rain splashing her face and the ugly brown paper over the windows hammering the truth home like a stake in her heart. She had to accept this and move on.

Turning, she trudged toward her own office, her legs shaking, needing sanctuary in the familiar, needing to be alone with her weary heart.

"Sunny! Wait."

She whipped around and saw Connor standing in the doorway to his office, a smile on his handsome face, his nut-brown hair appealingly disheveled, as usual. He stepped out onto the boardwalk and headed toward her, his head bent against the increasingly heavy rain.

Her breath caught in her throat and her heart started dancing a jig in her chest. Lord, she wished she wasn't so darned happy to see him.

He reached out and took her elbow. "Come out of the rain. I have something to show you." He urged her in the direction of his office.

She pulled back, digging in her heels. "No, Connor, I can't go in there."

He stopped, scowling. "Look, it's starting to pour. We can't talk out here."

"I don't want to talk at all." She just knew she'd break down if she was around him right now.

"Please?" he said, looking right at her, the plea mirrored in his green eyes. "It's important."

She peered at him through the rain. How smart was it to go with him when she was feeling so raw and emotional, when her heart ached just looking at him?

Rain had started to soak through her jacket and leather boots, chilling her to the bone, and she couldn't feel her face anymore. And, really, she'd waded through the most treacherous Connor waters yesterday, had put the most difficult decision of her life behind her. She was safe now, her heart unable to break any more, the inevitable acknowledged and accepted. Her gaze strayed to his office window. The brown paper said it all. She and Connor were over.

"Okay," she managed to say, wiping the rain out of her eyes. "But just for a minute."

He took her hand in his large, amazingly warm one and led her into his office. She held on, savoring his touch one last time.

She froze when she stepped inside. The wall between their two offices had been torn down, the rubble still surrounding the place where the wall had once stood. "What's going on?"

Connor came to stand in front of her. "I knocked down the wall."

She rolled her eyes. "I can see that." Stepping forward, she assessed the larger space, thinking about how odd it was for the physical barrier between his professional world and hers to be gone. "Why?"

"Because I want you to be my partner."

She pulled in her chin and gave him a puzzled look. "That would be a little hard for you to do from California, wouldn't it?"

"I'm not leaving."

She looked at him to see if he was joking, but his mouth was pulled into a stiff line. He was serious. Elation quickly rose inside of her but she ruthlessly squashed it down. "Uh, why not?" she asked, intensely curious about his change of heart, even though she refused to get her hopes up and believe it had anything to do with her, only to be painfully slapped back down again. He might be staying, but that was as far as it went. This was nothing more than him deciding her methods had value, a professional nod. While that was a good thing on one level, it hardly healed her ailing heart.

He shrugged one broad shoulder. "I changed my mind, decided I wanted to work here, with you."

His words landed like sharp spikes inside of her, tearing her up. This was all about work, not what lived in his heart or, in this case, what *didn't* live in his heart—any love for her.

She looked at him, her eyes burning, hear heart shattering all over again. "No, Connor."

"Tell me why not," he said, coming over and grasping her shoulders, looking right into her eyes. "I want to know."

She searched the face of the man she loved, seeing his honesty and integrity in every line of his face and every facet of his deep green eyes. She owed him the truth even if he never returned her love, even if it hurt her to admit it when he wouldn't be saying the same words back.

And this…thing with Connor needed to be finished today so she could gain closure, move on, fulfill the pact and build the committed, stable life she wanted. She took a deep breath, steeling herself to admit her deepest, most revealing feelings. "It will never be enough to simply be your business partner."

She pulled away and turned from him, wrapping her

arms around her waist, feeling achy and chilled and so very alone. "I love you," she whispered, her throat tight. "It would be torture to work with you when you don't love me, or worse yet, have to watch you leave town without me some day. That would be more than I could bear." Hot tears crested and ran down her cheeks.

After a long, silent moment, she heard what sounded like paper rustling. But she kept her head bent and didn't turn around, ashamed of breaking down when it seemed easy for Connor to stay in perfect control, for him to hold himself aloof when she was crumbling inside.

Connor came up behind her and gently placed his arms around her waist, pulling her close. He bent and planted a tender kiss on her right temple, his whiskers rasping against her skin, making her heart skip a beat, suffusing her in heat and the sheer contentedness she always felt when he was near. Then he whispered in her ear, "Turn around, Sunny," urging her around with his arms.

She reluctantly did as he asked, looking at the floor, trying to control the moisture pouring from her eyes and not come undone and sob like a baby. When she was facing the other way, she looked up.

The paper was gone from the window, revealing a new, more colorful sign painted on the glass. She peered at the words. Though the letters were backward, it didn't take long for her to figure out what they said.

MR. AND MRS. COMMITMENT.

Her stomach dropped and a cold chill ran up her spine. She pulled away so she could turn around and look at Connor, her eyes wide and her mouth hanging open to the point she could barely speak. "Wh…what does this mean?" she asked, her eyes brimming with tears again, desperately needing to hear the words before she'd let herself believe anything.

He reached for her, a new emotion shining from his eyes—oh, good gracious, was it love?—pulling her snug against his big, warm, masculine body. He lowered his head and kissed her tenderly, reverently, before he pulled away slightly, smoothing her damp hair back from her face, staring deep into her eyes. "It means that I can't live without you." He kissed both of her eyes, then her mouth, his lips soft and compelling. "I love you Sunny," he said between kisses, "and I want you to be my partner in life, too. *You're* my dream, not some stuffy job." He lifted his head. "I was a fool to think I could walk away from you when I love you so much. Marry me."

Pure, brilliant joy tumbled through Sunny, lighting up all the shadowed places in her heart, making it full and whole. Miraculously, Connor the Noncommitted had fallen in love with her. One burning question remained, though. "What happened?" she asked, curious about how he'd made such a dramatic turnaround. "What changed your mind?"

He shook his head ruefully, his eyes glinting. "You did."

She frowned. "I did? How?"

He bent and kissed her nose. "Other than being my one true love?" he asked with a playful lift of one brow. At her quick, ecstatic nod, he continued. "By showing me that I was able to function in a personal relationship. You're pretty smart, you know. That bit of news got me to thinking, and I determined that if I was so afraid of failing, letting a wonderful, amazing, perfect woman like you walk away would be the ultimate failure." He shrugged, his eyes alight with happiness. "Hey, I'm a practical guy, and I hate failing, you know, so I did the only thing I could—I hustled my butt down here, met the sign painter, ripped down the wall and prepared my case."

She smiled up at the man she loved, her faith in karma, and true love, restored. "You've made an offer I can't possibly refuse, Mr. Commitment. Of course I'll marry you."

Her teary, happy gaze catching on the new sign, she pulled Connor's head down for another tender kiss, never wanting to let him go, ecstatic that she wouldn't have to after all. He was hers. Forever.

She'd finally found the perfect man and the perfect job and a commitment that would last forever.

What more could she possibly ask for?

* * * * *

COMING NEXT MONTH

#1750 ENGAGED TO THE SHEIK—Sue Swift
In a Fairy Tale World...

Expert heartbreaker Selina Carrington isn't about to fall prey
to Kamar ibn Asad's legendary charm. Yet with every moment
she spends pretending to be engaged to the charismatic sheik—
romantic dinners and moonlit walks on the beach included—
she becomes more and more enchanted by his soulful eyes and
whispered promises....

#1751 THE BOSS, THE BABY AND ME—Raye Morgan
Boardroom Brides

Jodie Allman only trusts her handsome new boss as far as
she can throw him! An ancient feud between their families
makes her suspicious of Kurt McLaughlin's position with
Allman Industries. But as they get down to business, Jodie
might decide that it's time to try to mend fences with the
McLaughlins...and the sexy single dad who's captured her
heart.

#1752 THE SUBSTITUTE FIANCÉE—Rebecca Russell

Mac McKenna is marrying the wrong twin! And when Plain-
Jane Jessie Taggert stands in for her glamorous, but freaked-out
sister, sparks fly between the hunky groom and his fill-in
fiancée. What will Mac do when faced with the choice to do
his duty by one sister or follow his heart into the arms of the
other?

#1753 A RING AND A RAINBOW—Deanna Talcott

As childhood sweethearts, Hunter Starnes and Claire Dent
were inseparable. If only that had lasted! Now Hunter's back
in town to sell his family home, and he can't help but be drawn
to the one woman who made him feel complete. Maybe Claire
can help the lonely tycoon find love—and a wedding ring—at
the end of a rainbow.

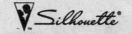